S0-CFB-063

The Hammer

By Jason Trench

THE HAMMER
THE TYPESCRIPT

The Hammer

JASON TRENCH

EAST CHICAGO PUBLIC LIBRARY
EAST CHICAGO, INDIANA

A CRIME CLUB BOOK
Doubleday
NEW YORK LONDON TORONTO SYDNEY AUCKLAND

MAI 236 9/8 1

A Crime Club Book
Published by Doubleday, a division of
Bantam Doubleday Dell Publishing Group, Inc.
666 Fifth Avenue, New York, New York 10103

Doubleday and the portrayal of a man
with a gun are trademarks of
Doubleday, a division of Bantam Doubleday Dell
Publishing Group, Inc.

All of the characters in this book
are fictitious, and any resemblance
to actual persons, living or dead,
is purely coincidental.

Library of Congress Cataloging-in-Publication Data
Trench, Jason.
The Hammer / Jason Trench.
p.   cm.
"A Crime Club novel."
I. Title.
PR6070.R3665H36   1989
823'.914—dc19   88-35608
CIP
ISBN 0385-26251-5

Copyright © 1989 by Jason Trench
All Rights Reserved
Printed in the United States of America
August 1989

F
T7918h

The Hammer

"Leaving already?" I asked, a trifle more sharply than I had intended. I'd always believed that, when it came to office discipline, being understated was best.

Edwina Murphy, our newest typist, was pert and very pretty, with round pink cheeks that seemed perpetually flushed, as though she had been running or caught in the act of doing something she shouldn't. She hesitated. "It's only ten to. Is there anything else you want me to do?"

She nearly caught me off guard there. It was what I didn't altogether like about the younger generation. They weren't averse to answering back. Or at least they weren't when they had just joined the office, and Edwina had joined only the previous month. Usually they got into the way of doing things after six months or so. Either that, or they didn't stay, I thought ruefully. I thought quickly. "I was just going to ask you to type these three letters." Actually I wasn't and there was nothing urgent about them; she had just got on the wrong side of me, when she made to leave early. "Then you can go," I added kindly. A flash of anger crossed her face, then she picked up the letters and went back to her desk, taking off her jacket rather ostentatiously.

"Can't they wait until morning, Harry? It's not

anything to do with the Sempleton contract, is it? Nothing else is urgent." The tones were the rather jangling, immature ones of young Palmer. I pursed my lips. I had liked the young lad well enough when he had joined at the age of eighteen. He had been polite and deferential then. Now he was twenty-one, he had turned cheeky and—worse still —had begun to talk to me as though I was his employee, not his father's. The boy nominally was a partner of course, as I was. But I had put the firm on its feet, together with Arthur Palmer, who had provided the capital and many of the contacts. It irritated me, the way the son spoke to me. I was in charge of the day-to-day running, he did the selling, taking people to visit properties and so on, together with the two young men the firm now employed. In any other office, he would respect my seniority. But I couldn't say so, of course, because that would have upset Arthur.

He had no call to criticise me with others present, though. "They won't take long," I said crisply. He sighed. I was conscious they had exchanged exasperated looks, and then it dawned on me that there was something between them. That wouldn't do at all: young Palmer should not allow his personal involvements to get in the way of work. I frowned, pretending to be absorbed in papers. On the dot of five Palmer strode to the door. Edwina took until ten past to finish the letters, and then gave them to me. "Thank you," I said. "Have a pleasant evening."

"Good night," was all she said. I tidied up my desk, checked the safe was locked, turned out the lights and left. I closed the door carefully, locking it. A police car, its red lights shut off, drifted off down the street. You saw a lot of police cars these days in Farleigh, wasting ratepayers' money. I walked down the road to where my Ford Anglia was parked and climbed in. I drew satisfaction from the way it whirred into action as soon as I switched on the ignition. It wasn't a BMW, but it served me perfectly, reliably. It was just right for my speed, for my stroll through life. I didn't believe in killing myself, unlike some of those young tearaways you saw around.

Turning off the high street, the road climbed to where narrow terrace houses huddled in frightened rows on the side of the hill the town was built against. There was no traffic about, hardly a passerby even. Another police car was stationed silently in Ryder Street. I felt less than reassured. I wondered whether they were noting down the numbers of passing vehicles in and out of the red-light area. Next time, perhaps I should leave the car at the office and pick it up on the way home. One couldn't be too cautious where sparing Mummy was concerned. Still, though, they would have seen me by now. They couldn't follow up everyone who went into the Jericho district, surely? Or could they? The police were desperate, according to the newspapers.

I parked the car three houses away from my destination; there were no police in Querchmore Road, no one at all, in fact. Only eight months ago there had been four or five girls walking the kerbside. That was where I had picked up Eileen, as casually as that. Now it had developed into something bigger than I had anticipated. . . .

I opened the little wrought iron gate and walked down the short path to the wooden door with the coloured glass front panel. I rang the bell of Number 33 and surveyed the cold, tidy little garden, a patch of green surrounded by earth beds out of which poked sad skeletons of flowers. An eye peered through the spyhole and the door opened. Eileen was there, and I hurried in, suddenly weaker in the legs, as I always seemed to be with her. I couldn't understand why.

She was wearing her bright pink dressing gown over a plain white nightdress. I thought she looked a little paler than usual, under the powder and the rouge and the dark eyeliner she always put on for my benefit. She had smiled briefly as I came in, but it wasn't her warm smile, it was the one she had on when she was preoccupied.

She almost pushed me up the stairs, to the bedroom; another of the girls, Fleur, was filling the kettle from the tap on the landing. She smiled hello. I was embarrassed. I always was when I met another of the girls.

In the room I took off my raincoat. Eileen went to pour me a glass of sherry from her little cabinet by the big chest of drawers. It was a small room—only just large enough for the bed and a slightly battered-looking secondhand chair and a washstand and the chest of drawers. The bed was big though, and old fashioned, like the one I slept in at home, with a sturdy brass head and base; it was comfortable, the kind of bed you wouldn't roll out of.

She lit herself a cigarette—it was the one thing I couldn't stand about her, her chain-smoking—and

handed me the drink. She looked at me. I thought
her eyes were sad and her hands nervous as she
puffed away at her cigarette. She put out her two
hands and undid my tie, as she always did. I swallowed, as I always did. She was the only woman
who had ever touched me, undressed me, apart
from Mummy. I sat very still as she pulled the tie
off from around my neck and then eased the jacket
off my back, and then began to undo the buttons on
my shirt, leading down to the bulge—I admit it—of
a tummy that was overweight from all Mummy's
cooking. All the time I watched the low cut of
Eileen's nightdress, as she tilted towards me, the
nipples on her bosoms showing.

She didn't take my shirt off when she finished
unbuttoning it, just ran her hands up and down
inside it. I remember the first time she did that, it
seemed unbelievable that any woman wouldn't
shrink at the touch of my body. But she had smiled
that time, as though enjoying it, and even though I
was paying for it, I believed afterwards that she
had enjoyed it.

She got up, still in front of me, as she always did,
and removed her dressing gown, and then lifted
her nightdress quite unconcernedly and stood before me without a stitch on. I peered at her a little
sheepishly through my horn-rimmed glasses, and
then leaned forward to feel her curves. She turned
round, as she always did, and I gave her a few gentle pats on her behind. She never allowed me more
than three or four of these—they were quite gentle,
mind—and then she turned around with that alluring look of hers and asked me to take off all of my
clothes. I switched off the light and did so, quickly

and sheepishly. When I was seated again on the
bed, I could feel her hand. It was very gentle, and
very, very persuasive. Then she sat astride me, and
I could feel her command, her guidance. In the
half-light I glimpsed her towering body. It was under her control that I experienced that lovely sensation and then the sadness and tiredness. Never
mind: it was something I absolutely had to have, I
had realised that ever since I had it the first time
with her.

After that I lay beside her, a little frightened. She
was warm and soothing, and it felt nice just to be
in contact with her lovely smooth skin. She gave
me fifteen minutes of that. Then she switched on
the light and I felt exposed. I got under the blankets. She lit another cigarette and didn't look at me.
She said: "There's something I've got to talk to you
about." She hesitated. "You'll have to make it a little more this time."

I was used to that, to her little mores: when she
was short, I'd give her a pound or two extra, on top
of the usual ten pounds. She did me so well, and I
wanted to show she was special to me. I knew from
the special attentions she gave me that she liked
me, that the money wasn't the reason. But she had
to live, like anyone else. I said: "That's all right.
But not regularly, mind you."

"A lot more," she said. The little glow in the
dark and the smoke obscured the outline of her
head. "I didn't tell you, I've got a husband."

I was astonished. I didn't say anything. "He's
been picked up on a charge—breaking and entering. He's up before the beak on Tuesday. He's on a
suspended sentence. He'll get three years. I've got

to get him bailed, just so I can see him before it happens."

"You never told me you were married," I said peevishly.

"Oh, he don't mean anything to me," she said, quickly. "You're the one, Harry. . . . My life changed when you came into it. I mean that. But I got a duty. You can understand that, can't you? We're not even really married. I'm just— He's Ginny's father." Ginny was Eileen's four-year-old daughter, who was in care.

"But how much are you talking about? I haven't got any money." I was getting cross.

"You can take it from the office. You look after its money, don't you?"

I was firm now. I had my shirt on, and my dignity was returning. "Don't ever speak of such a thing again. It's the most disgraceful suggestion I've ever heard."

But she wasn't frightened of me. She didn't seem worried that she had made me upset. Her eyes were rather blank. "Perhaps your mother's got the money. Perhaps you could ask her. Or I could."

The little fool. Didn't she realise what it would do to Mummy even to know that I was acquainted with someone like her?

But she did. I was just being slow. She said, "Harry I'm desperate. And I'll do anything to get him out. I'm sorry."

And then I saw what she was really saying, and the wind went out of me. I just stared at her, that little strumpet, and she looked levelly at me, and my anger was doubled. "You won't get a penny out of me," I hissed, between my teeth. I grabbed my raincoat and stalked angrily out, banging the door behind me.

I slammed the front door too. I heard a window being raised from the upper floor. "You've got two days, or I go to your mother," she shouted. It was a fishwife's voice. I couldn't believe I had ever been taken in by someone like her. I glanced nervously over my shoulder in the dark, in case anyone had noticed the rumpus. But there was no one on the street, and I drove the car home, down the hill, past the terraced houses of the red-light area, past the police car, in a sweat of fury and nerves.

Mummy could see I wasn't myself when I returned and ascended past the formal sitting and dining room we never used, to the living room. She had her feet up on her rest, watching television. The sitting room was about ninety degrees; I switched off the gasfire. "It's cooking in here," I told her tetchily. "We're burning up money. Just burning it up. I'm not made of it. How many times do I have to tell you that?"

"Not even your good evening kiss, dear?" she asked. I gave a snort and went over to where she was sunk into the chair, her blankets wrapped around her. I gave the still remarkably smooth cheek a kiss. She had preserved an astonishing skin, although the wrinkles around her eyes and her neck were deep. Her careful diet had something to do with it. "I've had my dinner," she told me. "But I've made you a lovely Hungarian goulash. It's on the stove."

"Thank you very much, Mummy." But I wasn't in the mood for eating. I went and fetched the food and came back into the room to watch the televi-

sion while I ate it. I sat beside her. A sense of security returned as I gazed round the furnished room,
the pivot of my life since Daddy had died sixteen
years before, and I had taken over looking after
Mummy. She needed someone to be with her, she
was so badly alone after his death. And yet— I
might have been leading a little brood of children
through the park if it had been otherwise.

I sighed with relief: I was lucky. I couldn't imagine any fate worse than to have had little brats
screaming and being mischievous, and a shrewish
wife angry at me. Mummy wasn't like that. She
never shouted, although she could be tetchy sometimes. But I knew how to get her out of those
moods.

The room was Mummy's taste, with its comfortable faded armchairs, the unsmiling picture of her
grandfather with a beard on the wall, the familiar
naval prints and the Victorian print of a naughty
little girl. The ornate lampstand and the heavy
black furniture were hers too, and so was the little
silver-plated drinks tray and the silver-plate teapot
that glistened on the dining room table where we
always ate on Sundays. I found myself wondering
how much they were worth, then mentally
checked myself.

"Are you sure you're quite right?" she said. Her
voice had grown older in the last couple of years; it
had a tremor to it, although it remained as strong
and as clear as ever. She had been a little more
sedentary, too, not going out so much, preferring
the same chair in the sitting room. She had had a
fright when the doctor told her she had angina, and
had told her to cut down on the unstoppable en-

ergy of her earlier years. I almost preferred her
now, when she was less talkative, less formidable,
more dependent on me. "Stop fussing, mother," I
told her.

"Very well. Take no notice of what I say. It's just
me, as usual. But is there something wrong,
Harry?" Her eyes were pools of anxiety, no longer
looking at the television set. I stared ahead.

"I said there wasn't, didn't I?"

She sighed. "Is it something to do with the office?"

"It's nothing to do with the office," I said
sharply.

"With the Society then." My recreation was the
local history society. I had been its secretary for
eight years. It gave us great enjoyment, investigat-
ing the history of the area and hiring occasional
speakers. We used to drink a little vintage port at
our gatherings, which sometimes became very
merry. Lately, though, a younger man, a twenty-
seven-year-old history lecturer at the polytechnic,
had been trying to get the post from me. I certainly
wasn't too old at thirty-eight, and the job needed
expertise. He was one of those new style of historians who believed in social research, and wanted to
reorient our studies towards "living history"—in-
terviewing a lot of old men to find out what the
town was like in their youth. It was stuff and nonsense: we turned to history to get away from the
horrors of modern life and society. The purpose of
the club was a social one, not political. All the
same, one or two of our members seemed to have
been taken in by him. He was dreadfully energetic,
a little man with frizzed up hair and spectacles and

the horrible jargon of someone brought up since education went wrong. "Has whatshisname—Pallance—taken over the club?" she asked pointedly.

"Of course not," I snapped.

"It's just you're so much on edge. What is it, then?"

I wanted to tell her to be quiet. But I knew it wouldn't do; it wouldn't satisfy her, or stop her. So I tossed her a bone. "Young Palmer was furious with me because I told him off for flirting with one of the secretaries. He said he would try to get me sacked. Of course it won't happen. His father won't listen to the boy. But it's upsetting. And he was playing around with that girl in the office, when he was already late for two flat-showing appointments. It was very upsetting." I repeated.

She came over to where I was sitting. She sat on the arm of the chair and stroked my cheek. "Poor darling. Poor boy. I wish I could make it better."

"Honestly, Mummy, I'm not a child," I said, not unkindly. "I'll get a drink for both of us." I busied myself with the tray.

"Just a very weak whisky for me," she said, and I gave her her usual half and half.

She was appeased by the offering and believed the story. I often had to make up stories for her, to placate her whenever I had a real difficulty, because I didn't want to worry her with it, or have her offer me some of her infuriating advice. She would consider it a personal slight if I didn't follow it. This time, though, it was different. She had always disapproved of my few girlfriends or been critical of them. I remember at one party which a friend of mine from school had held, I had seen the most lovely girl. She had fairly swept me off my feet, and unusually, talked to me when I talked to her. I arranged to meet her two days later.

I could see I was upsetting mother when I told her, and when the young lady actually came to visit, she was heartily disapproved of. That happened a couple of times. Of course I blamed Mummy in some ways for wrecking my love life. But the decision to live with her was entirely mine, and I loved her more than I would any passing fancy: I wanted to go on living with her. Who would look after her otherwise? I was an only son. Life with Mummy was quiet, but it was pleasant and predictable. I hated unpredictability. And there was plenty of variety in the work: every day brought new challenges in the office—a chain of house sales depending on each other would fall through, or one would succeed—no one could say the business was an unexciting one.

So what had made me go down Ryder Street, that street of shame? The fleeting images on the television screen in front of me went unseen; my thoughts were miles away. I remembered how over the years I had envied the young men in the office and in the history circle and in the pubs I frequented. I envied them for their girlfriends. I hated women because I didn't understand them and they showed no interest in me, but clearly some men did, and I envied them. And I had so much—so much of that feeling I hardly dared admit within me—desire. Why shouldn't I have a little enjoyment of that kind, try it out?

So I went in search of someone, and one of the women on the street accosted me, and came up to me because I was afraid to go up to her. I had to walk past her two times before she did. She was good-looking and she was friendly. She was very gentle to begin with, because I was so frightened and unused to it. And now look where it had led me.

I did a lot more drinking than usual that evening, and I saw my mother looking at me curiously when I went to bed before she did, which was very unusual.

I tried to put the problem out of my mind the next day, and almost succeeded. It was the Thursday, the day on which Eileen had threatened to tell Mummy, that the worry returned again. I had control over office finances and had the authority to remove money from the account at my own discretion. No one would find out, for a while; I was absolutely trusted. I could probably get away with it, too. Old Palmer was getting too old to notice such things and young Palmer preferred me to do the work. I could put it down as a surveying fee, or some such. But I couldn't. It would be a betrayal of everything I had worked for, of all of my values. I was trusted, and could not break that trust. Besides, if I gave her some now, she would come back for more. Remember what they said about the Dane and the Danegeld? She was a rotten little crook as well as a slut, and I blamed myself for submitting to her bodily temptations. Wasn't this fitting punishment? Wasn't this just retaliation for indulging in such filthy acts with a common garden whore? And if Mummy found out, it would kill her. . . . She had an exalted view of me, and I was central to her whole being. Imagine if that woman came to her to tell her we made love! She wouldn't understand that I had just been using her, using her for sex, that was all. What an ugly little word it was.

I went out at lunch and bought a pint of beer and read a paper to calm my nerves. The latest police botch-up in the Hammer hunt was blazoned across the front page. Apparently they had cordoned off the red-light district around Ryder Street, where they thought a murder might take place, three weeks earlier. The murder had duly taken place and the Hammer had duly slipped through. My regard for policemen was not very high.

But the story held my attention only momentarily. My mind had been going around in circles, wondering what to do. Surely she wouldn't go through with it? She wouldn't get what she wanted by telling my mother—unless she did it out of spite. Perhaps I should go and see her again, impress on her the futility of it. But now I hated her so, I might lose control of myself. And anyway she would see it as an indication of weakness, as a sign that I was desperate, that I could be forced to get the money after all. In the end I resolved to do no other than to watch and wait outside the house, where she would have to pass, in case she did try to approach. I didn't want her ringing the doorbell, even. My mother would ask what it was all about.

I excused myself early from the office, which raised eyebrows but aroused no comments. I was the one person who kept absolutely strict hours in the office, apart from the secretaries. I drove up through the grey streets, where the houses were

grouped together like a long gauntlet, darkened
and secretive and, for the first time, I thought, a
little forbidding, as though people were watching
me to see what I would do, how I would react to
the scandal bursting out and my name being
dragged in the mud—even though we had such a
small circle of friends. It was raining, and a light
patter drummed on the car windscreen and gave
the road a sheen. There was no one about, even so
early in the evening.

It was hard to stop directly in front of the house,
because the road was a dual carriageway and there
was nowhere to stop (we had got used to the noise
over twenty-six years of living there). But I could
see down the road well enough from just around
the corner, by the post office. Everyone knew me
there. I hoped that no one would observe the curious spectacle of me spying on my own house. I
shrank in my seat, and listened to the rain on the
roof. I got slowly colder after the engine had been
switched off.

I determined that if nothing had happened by
half past nine, I would go into the house. Of
course, she might have come already. But I doubted
it. Eileen would have waited for me, as always, to
come back from work on a Thursday. She wouldn't
wait too long, though, because she might lose the
best part of the evening, the nine-thirty to twelve
period, when the pubs closed. I had thought it all
out in my mind, again and again, that day.

Then I saw her. She was moving rather fast
through the rain, holding an umbrella. She would
always think of something like that so as not to
disarrange her profitable looks. She seemed ner-

vous, and I didn't wonder, with that monster on the loose. I had hardly seen a woman alone on the streets in months. I switched the engine on and the car slid forwards; on foot I couldn't have caught her before she had reached the house, she was walking so fast. I was sweating and trembling all over. The car slid across, turning into the main road, and came up beside her. Even so I was only just in time. She had reached the garden gate. The bitch. The bitch! She had come after all, to try and ruin me and drive my mother to an early grave out of pure blackmailer's spite.

She started, as my Anglia slowed beside her. "You had better jump in," I said. Relief flooded her face when she recognised me. I had really underestimated how much fear of the Hammer had affected all the people of the area.

She hesitated an instant. She was wearing a long raincoat over her usual short skirt, perhaps to make her profession less obvious. "I was going to see your mother."

"Do you want to hear what I have to say first?"

She shrugged. I could see she hoped I might have had something for her. She climbed in. I didn't really know what to do, or to say. I was sweating profusely. I couldn't even bear to look her in the face. I just wanted to get her away from my home.

She said, rather quietly, "Well, have you got the money?"

"No," I said, through clenched teeth. "No, I couldn't."

"Then what is there to talk about?" she said flatly.

"I'm taking you back to the flat. I never want you to come near my house again."

She laughed, and what I used to think was a gentle, sympathetic laugh sounded harsh and sarcastic, getting on my nerves. "How can anyone stop me? There'll always be a time when you aren't there, waiting, watching me with those horrid little eyes of yours, greedy eyes, waiting for me to undress. Little pig eyes . . ."

My eyes flooded with tears of fury. I jammed my foot on the brake, and turned and slapped her as hard as I could, which wasn't very hard, with the palm of my hand. She screamed. "Let me out. Let me out of this car, you—you pervert!" She wrenched the door open and attempted to plunge out.

I grabbed her by the arm. "Wait!" I told her. I managed to half pull her back inside and she turned back to me: her mascara was smudged, her hair was plastered loosely across her forehead, her eyes were ablaze with ugly anger. "Swear never to come near my house again. Swear it." I barked. I didn't know I was capable of such fury.

"Or you'll what, you little pervert?" she spat out.

"Swear it!" I demanded and held her harder. She couldn't break free.

"Let me go! Let me go! Help!" she began yelling. The noise was so loud I feared it would attract attention, and I let go in my fluster of worry. When I jumped out of the car, I saw her backing off, down the street. "I'll be there tomorrow and after tomorrow and after that, watching by your mother's house, waiting to tell her that her beloved son's a pervert," she hissed to me.

"You do that and see what happens to you," I said, moving towards her.

"What? What?" she taunted. I was near enough to grab her now, and I made a lunge, but I missed. She screamed again, and started running down the street. I ran after her; we were about evenly matched, her high heels and skirt keeping her from getting too far ahead of my rather overweight body; running was not one of my favourite activities. I puffed after her, as she rounded a corner.

As I reached it, I saw her slip off towards a patch of wasteland near a derelict building: she had no hope of escape that way. I plunged madly after her, and it nearly caused me serious injury: I couldn't see a thing on the rough ground, away from the streetlights, and I stubbed my foot on something hard and stumbled.

That was what saved me: as I lurched sideways a blow struck me hard on the shoulder: I sank to my knees. As I staggered back to my feet, I realised the pain in my shoulder came from a brick she had thrown at me. I could hardly move my arm. She was standing, smiling at me, not five yards away. I could see the satisfaction in her face, through my misted spectacles, through my eyes smarting with pain.

And then it happened, something which had never happened before with me, no matter how crabby Mummy could be. A wild surge of anger possessed me, seeming to flow through the whole of my being to my brain. This little tart had taken my money, had tried to blackmail me, had tried to injure me, and now was laughing at me. I was incensed, almost beyond measure. I wanted to throttle her, hurt her with everything I had, frighten the living daylights out of her. I was out of control: the rage had taken hold of my mind, and my arms.

I sprang at her, and caught her by the shoulder as she turned to run. She tripped and fell sideways, rather awkwardly, then backwards over her own bent legs, and then there was an extraordinary crunch, something you couldn't describe unless you heard it, rather like the breaking of a large eggshell. I knew what had happened almost in that instant, yet my mind refused to accept it, and made me stumble to my knees beside her in the hope that it hadn't happened.

I grabbed hold of her, and to my horror she was limp. "Eileen," I whispered, shaking her. I could make out her face and shape in the dark now, and there was something odd about the shape of her head, and now that I could see her eyes, they were quite open. So she was all right, just looking at me in a horrified sort of way.

I shook her again, to get her out of her trance. "For God's sake," I said, but she was still looking at me in the same sort of way. I was sobbing with fright now. "Please speak to me, you silly girl. I'm sorry." But she was still looking, and I turned away under that merciless stare.

I got up and I stumbled away. She must be pretending, or perhaps she was in some sort of coma. I backed away to the nearby wall, from where she wasn't more than a darker patch huddled up against the blackness of the rubble-strewn building site. I pushed hard against the wall, as though trying to find a hole in it. I stayed motionless there for some time, and every few moments my gaze would be drawn back to the black patch on the ground. I was trembling and sweating and sobbing, and it must have been fully ten minutes, until the bitter, damp cold of the evening had reached deep into my bones, before my sense of reason returned.

It forced me forward, again, towards the shape on the ground. With icy self-control, I forced myself to kneel once again and take her hand. But it wasn't all that warm. I whispered "Eileen," and no answer came. I looked again into the sightless eyes. My hand found its way to her cooling forehead, through the hair. Gingerly I felt the top of her head. The hair was sticky there. I pulled my hand away where the head felt suddenly concave. In the half-light, I could see what had done it: a jagged broken brick, four inches away, sharp and angular and uncompromising against the delicate shell of a falling head. I still couldn't believe it.

I climbed to my feet in that desolate place, a half-empty expanse of broken bricks and old rubbish, dumped thoughtlessly from the road. A tossed-away human now lay in the middle of it. It looked pathetic. One moment it had been so full of venom and life and danger, now it was just a small, crumpled heap in a neglected corner, its limbs askew, lifeless like an old rag doll.

I don't know how long I stayed huddled there; but it was long after the cold had penetrated my sweat-soaked clothes once again and chilled my body to near-paralysis. My teeth were chattering. My whole face was trembling like half-formed jelly. I was just rooted to the horror and insignificance of it all. It wasn't so much for her—I couldn't care less for her, even now I couldn't summon an ounce of compassion for her. She had been trying to do an ugly thing, and had met an accident. After all, she had tried to kill me—or at any rate to injure me—with the brick. It was the knowledge that somehow my life had passed a watershed; things could never be the same again. I was entering into the realm of the great unknown, where I was never to know security, where I would never be able to forget this scene. Such an insignificant act, just attempting to grab her, had been turned by fate into the end of her and a crossroads for me. She was dead, and I was responsible. Of course I wasn't really—it had been an accident. But I would be held responsible.

It was that thought that awoke me from my paralysis. I looked nervously about. But the building site was well shielded from the road. Few people went for walks along the dual carriageway. On one side was a row of terraced cottages due for demolition; on the other a small, closed electrical spares shop. Behind, there was only a grassy slope. I looked at my watch. Just four minutes past seven, yet it had seemed like a lifetime. I moved slowly, reluctantly away from the scene, a horrified fascination compelling me to look back. I had some wild idea that I should wipe my fingerprints off the body, but I knew I wouldn't even know how to begin. I peered warily over the rubble at the edge of the building site and looked down the road. Not a soul could be seen. There were four cars parked there: my own, and behind it a Ford Cortina, a small Austin Allegro and—my heart jumped—a police car, with its lights out.

I stood there, rooted to the spot, every nerve in

my body aching with tension. My heart was beating like a steamhammer, and I could feel the sweat trickling down the inside of my shirt. They must have been just watching me, observing, because there was no movement and the lights didn't come on. Why didn't they get it over with and drive down and pick me up? They had all the evidence they needed. My hands were still sticky with her blood.

Cars raced up and down the dual carriageway, a flurry of unseeing speed and sound and headlights, and I stood just out of range of them, watching. Then the thought occurred that they hadn't seen me, perhaps they were there by chance. The area was always crawling with police. But it was too much to hope. Regaining an iron control over myself, I began to move forward, entering the space under the streetlight that towered over my car. No, they were there all right. I had the distinct, prickly feeling I was being watched.

There was nothing for it but to keep my nerve. I unlocked the car as coolly as I could, opened the door slowly—to give them time to come and pick me up—then got in. The Anglia started first go. My feet were trembling so much on the clutch and the accelerator I hardly trusted myself to pull out. I watched in the mirror, but they didn't follow.

I couldn't go home, not straight away, not in my present state. Even if I managed to clean my hands, Mummy would notice the state I was in, and I didn't trust myself not to blurt it all out because I desperately wanted to talk to someone—anyone—but of course I couldn't. I turned the car up towards the moor, towards the village of Princetown, a bleak little former mining community which perched precariously on the edge of the climb. I wanted to get out and away from the claustrophobic town below, to think. I had an uneasy feeling I was being followed, and I checked again and again in the mirror, but there was no sign of the police. I knew that this was only one of the changes that tonight would have wrought in my life: I would never feel left alone again, but always be burdened by the fear that someone might find out. They probably would.

The car purred through the tired little shopping street of Princetown, with its grocery shops and ironmongers and post office, closed up and desolate and uninviting. The enamel rain hammered down on the windows and even the windscreen wipers had hard work clearing it away. It didn't matter because there was so little traffic about. Past the little greystone Methodist chapel, the road suddenly moved into open country, where there were only a few scattered, isolated small-holdings, little homesteads for men who had grown tired of the grime of city life and could afford only a cottage and a cow or two where no one else wanted them.

It was three or four minutes to the lip of the moor proper. I turned down a little lane I knew, where I used to go a great deal in my younger days; I stopped a mile or so down it, by a gate, which I climbed over. I went on down the sodden field in the dark to a stream, and I stumbled down the stones beside it until I could put my trembling hands into the icy cold water. I rubbed and rubbed them until I felt the layer of dried blood peel away.

I didn't think I had got any of it on my person. I walked back to the car and wiped the handle of the door and the driving wheel carefully with a cloth when I got back.

I stood beside it, and for the first time the tension began to leave me: with clean hands, I felt that a little of the horror of the day was receding. I breathed in the cold air of the moist wet fields, which felt fresh and invigorating in my lungs. A sudden deep tiredness was beginning to steal over me. I wanted to slump where I was, on the hillside; but I knew I had to think, think it out now, because by tomorrow—even by the time I got back this evening—it might be too late. They might be waiting for me down there, waiting to pick me up. If they were— My God, how would Mummy have taken it? Oh, how had I got myself into all this?

I turned the car round in the space by the gate, and drove back onto the main road. But instead of turning down to Princetown, I turned left onto the moor. I knew there was a pub, a bleak little place, a couple of miles further on. There I would have time to think, and I had long needed a drink. I turned in the little yard, where there were few cars parked. Outside I felt the brush of the cold air on my face with real pleasure again, and could hear a distant baaing of sheep. The sound of a stream tinkling in the stillness also gave me comfort.

I went into the bar, where a dour-faced barman fetched me a pint and tried to strike up a conversation about where I had just come from. I was hardly in the mood. I pocketed my change quickly, but gave him a smile, so as not to arouse his interest. I watched him walk down the bar to talk to one

of the regulars. They eyed me, but they probably
eyed any new face. I sat looking out over the little
brass ornaments and rudimentary little table and
chairs, and I considered the wreckage of my whole
life. With an effort, I applied my maxim at work:
every problem had a solution. Nothing was impos-
sible. It was just a question of a businesslike surveying of the options.

I could, first, go to the police and explain what
had happened. Explain that it had happened by accident: she had slipped and fallen, after she had
tried to throw a brick at me. After all, the evidence
fitted: her head had clearly been broken on the
brick. I struck that off my list at once. First, the
police wanted a suspect. Second, they would never
swallow a story like that. I had a good motive. I
could have hit her with the brick that had killed
her. If it was just a question of trusting to their
judgment about what happened in that yard that
night, I might as well forget it. I wouldn't convince
them, and I wouldn't convince a court. I would be
a squalid little man to them, indulging in my little
tart. Someone like that was more than capable of
bashing her brains out. They would take pleasure
in sending me to prison—there was nothing about
me that would instil compassion in them. I had always despised most of my fellow human beings,
and I believed that they despised me. Besides, the
whole ghastly affair with Eileen would come out
into the open if I were arrested and tried in court,
whether I was found guilty or acquitted. My job
would certainly be lost. Worse, I was sure that
Mummy wouldn't survive the shock. That option
was ruled out.

Secondly, there was the course of action that most often appealed to me. I could return home as though nothing had happened. Perhaps the police car hadn't noticed me. There was nothing to link me to her, except that my number was probably in her book of clients and that Fleur, who shared her flat, knew me. But Eileen had dozens of clients. There was no reason why I should be singled out. I probably would be: they would check on all of them, and Fleur would tell on me. They would surely come round to the house anyway. So it was better I went to them first, to prevent my mother from learning about it all. But they would wonder how I had got to know that she had been killed, unless I was the killer. It went round in my head, despairingly. And then I had a flash. I drained the glass, ordered another, and drank that at a gulp, leaving swiftly. The publican gave me a funny look, but I didn't care. I was in high spirits now, weaving the car back across the moor and down the hill.

They hadn't come yet. The house was in darkness. I rang the doorbell, and there was a long pause before the door opened. "Oh, it's you," said Fleur with a twinge of relief.

She was much younger than Eileen, maybe only nineteen; her face still had a flush of ruddy innocence about it, the genuine friendliness in her eyes hadn't yet hardened into the mould of the professional woman. She had her hair swept back from her face, quite short, leaving her forehead clear. She wasn't a great beauty, but the crinkles around her eyes and the cheeky turn of her mouth combined with the pert chin and slightly cherubic cheeks to make her attractive. I would have thought she would be a shop assistant with a steady boyfriend rather than—what she was. "It's no good," said Fleur with anxiety in her voice. "She isn't here."

"What do you mean?" I asked. "She should be expecting me."

"I don't know what's happened. She isn't usually so late. You always come on Tuesdays and Thursdays. She just said she had to go out and do something urgent. It was before six when she left."

"She's probably just been delayed. I'll wait in her room."

"She's never as late as this—and never late on the job." She was very anxious. "Oh, I wouldn't go in there," she said as I made for her room. I opened the door and had a shock. They had come already: Fleur had been bluffing. A burly, square-shouldered man with a moustache who was sitting on the bed looked up at me quizzically. I just stopped dead in the doorway. I said, stupidly, "Are you waiting for me?" and realised I had given it all away in my first words.

He climbed awkwardly to his feet, his face reddening. "No, for someone else. I think I'd better be off." Relief flooded back at me as I realised he meant her. He blundered out past me. I sat on the bed. Fleur came in and stood in the doorway. "I'm very worried," she said.

"Oh, she'll turn up," I said cheerfully.

She didn't. The police did. I heard the doorbell ring, and I heard Fleur's little cry when they identified themselves, and then something little short of a scream. They must have told her what had happened. They came blundering up the stairs. I jumped to my feet as the door opened. "I say— excuse me," I blustered.

The inspector was quite small, a tidy man with a moustache and level eyes and flecks of grey hair; I was surprised that he wore a grey anorak. There were two uniformed men and one woman police constable with him. They crowded into the little room. "What's this all about?" I asked in a low, embarrassed tone.

"First of all, sir, can you explain what you're doing here?"

"I'm waiting for a friend." I looked a little piqued.

"I see," he said dryly. "Would this friend by any chance be a Miss Eileen Dubois, nee Edwards, who I understand lives here?" I nodded. "You're going to have a long wait, I'm afraid. She's met with—an accident."

I stared at him dumbly. "Not a serious one, I hope?"

"I'm afraid so," he answered matter-of-factly. "I wonder if you'd oblige us sir, by answering a few questions. . . ." They asked me about my movements that night, whether there had been any witnesses to corroborate them. I told them I had stayed on a little later in the office than I had and that I had got to the pub a little earlier than I had. They wanted to know how long I had known Eileen, what sort of a person she was, whether she had been upset by anything recently, whether she was the kind of girl who took sensible precautions with regard to her own safety.

They took more than two hours, going very thoroughly and meticulously over every point. They weren't very alert, though, failing to follow up where my story seemed weakest. It was what I had always suspected about the police: they were obtuse.

Finally I said: "Officer, this is going on a long time."

Inspector Prescott looked up sharply. "Sir, you may as well know this is a murder enquiry. Everyone who knew her is under suspicion. That goes for the girl next door as well. Now, sir, I want to ask you this: what were you doing on the night of October 12 last?" There was a sudden tension in the room. The uniformed constables looked at me keenly. I had the impression that this was a very important question, although I hadn't the least idea why.

There was something familiar about the date. And then I remembered: that was the day I had read my paper to the History Society about the role of the gentry in Farleigh's development as an industrial town. I told them so. A perceptible flicker of disappointment crossed their faces. "And I assume there'll be witnesses to corroborate that?"

"There were eighteen people present, inspector."

"What time was that?"

"Oh, it always starts at around seven-thirty. But we ran on until eleven or so." The inspector looked at the constable and pursed his lips. He folded up his notebook. "Well, that's enough for now. Thank you for answering the questions so thoroughly. I

don't think we'll be troubling you further but
we've got your address just in case."

"I'd prefer you to contact me at the office if there
is anything, inspector. I've got an elderly
mother. . . ."

"I'll make a note of that, sir. And I'm sorry to
confirm that your lady friend here—there's no
harm in saying it now—has been murdered."

"Murdered." I allowed my eyebrows to rise, but
not by much. I was beginning to get used to the
part by now. "I hadn't imagined otherwise, from
the tone of the questioning. The lady in question
was—no more than an acquaintance. All the same,
I'm very sorry. Very sorry. Any idea who the killer
was?" I asked tentatively.

"An old friend," said the inspector with a smile,
and they left, leaving me to puzzle that one out.

It was all over the newspapers the following morning; there was the routine hideous mug shot of Eileen, and banner headlines: HAMMER'S NINTH HOR-
ROR; HAMMER STRIKES AGAIN.

I read the story without appearing too eager in
front of my mother. I was for a while absolutely
astonished: they were blaming him for it. Just because she was a prostitute. But—it was evident
from the story that the police had given out few
details of her murder. The injury to her head,
though, had unmistakably been caused by a small,
sharp instrument like a hammer. Other injuries
were characteristic of his kind of murder. I wondered what they meant by that. The story had a
photograph of Fleur—the journalists had got on to
her last night—and her recollection of how Eileen

had left that evening, how Fleur had told her to watch out, that no woman wandered the streets of Farleigh after dark. "If only she had listened," said Fleur. The police apparently had noticed nothing, as usual. The newspaper's editorial slammed them: "The failure to prevent yet another horrific crime is little short of a disgrace. Where were the police if not patrolling precisely this kind of ill-lit building site? How many more harmless—if not exactly innocent—women must die while the police sit on their haunches and this maniac goes free? As far as we can ascertain, the police, after eight months and around 21,000 hours of police work have no leads—not one."

In the car, on my way to work, I was struck by a sudden wave of euphoria. I was free. Yesterday hadn't been a turning point after all. By an extraordinary turn of fate, the police had taken her death to be the work of another man. And I suddenly recognised the significance of the question last night: now I remembered that the last Hammer murder had been committed between the hours of eight and nine on the night I had been giving my talk. As I had an alibi, I couldn't be the Hammer. And as the Hammer had killed Eileen, I couldn't be her murderer. I was free.

When I got to the office, young Palmer leered at me. "I see you were out on the town last night, Denman."

"What do you mean?"

"Another floozy got a bonk on the skull." He whooped with laughter, and I muttered an oath under my breath.

On Saturday I went to the public library, and took out the sheath of Hammer cuttings going back over eight months. I had become absorbed with the killings over the previous two days: it was a way of obliterating any remorse I might feel about her death, any sense of guilt. It had been an accident, I kept reminding myself. But how had the police got it so hopelessly wrong? I went meticulously through the local newspapers and the whole extraordinary coincidence struck me forcibly.

The injury to her skull had been remarkably like that of a Hammer victim. The motive was sexual, although the police had provided no specifics of the injuries that led them to that conclusion. That puzzled me: there was nothing sexual about the way Eileen had died, except her profession. The victims were almost exclusively prostitutes, except for number six, who was a student who had taken a short cut through the red-light district wearing a miniskirt and a rather loud jacket. The Hammer must have mistaken her for a prostitute. The police reckoned he was astonishingly cunning: although the murders occurred in a limited area, he never went to the type of location they expected he would after the previous murder. For example, if someone was killed on a patch of wasteland, the next victim would be found in a quiet spot just near a crowded pub, where no police would think of watching.

He was absolutely cool, absolutely deliberate, utterly merciless. No fingerprints were ever left, no identifiable trace of the man: murdering was his profession. He did it with skill and with calculation. He had terrorised the women of the town into staying at home after dark. Not being close to women other than my mother, I had failed to realise what an impact the killings had been having in Farleigh and a far wider area. Women were afraid to go out at all in the evenings, and the police presence had become a standard feature of the street scene. Yet I had barely noticed it, because neither I, nor any man, ever felt threatened. It was something one made the occasional joke about.

It was funny how Eileen exactly fitted the description of a typical victim. Mostly they were in their late twenties, the kind of girls who were so bold and in control that they felt they could brave down even a killer, and besides who needed the money before their looks faded. She even had physical similarities: she was a brunette, as were seven of the eight victims. She was smallish, which meant that a man of medium stature would find it easy to attack her. She wore a miniskirt, like all of the other victims. The psychologists believed this had enormous significance in providing an insight into the killer's mind, but I had never seen a prostitute who didn't wear a miniskirt. The man's ability to elude the police was also astonishing: twice he had killed within 100 yards of a police car and once on a beat being patrolled by a bobby. No one saw or heard anything. The newspapers claimed that a police car had been parked near the scene of Eileen's murder; but it had been empty. I wondered if the patrolmen had been having a quick snack somewhere.

The body had been discovered by a building worker, who at first had mistaken it for a bundle of clothing, so casually did it seem tossed aside in the

wasteland, from a distance. I felt no pity or remorse for her, but the awfulness of having extinguished a human life still held me in thrall. I felt as
though I had joined some terrible club of which the
Hammer was president.

My fascination with the case, and my interest in
history, led me naturally to read up about earlier
mass murders of this kind. The Jack the Ripper
case was the obvious parallel; there had been so
many rippers since then, though, that I imagined
that was why the headline writers had coined a
new name for this case: The Hammer Horror. I
became more and more convinced, as I read the
books about the Ripper case, that this murderer
was a literate man, perhaps even with a higher education, who knew his history and had consciously
modelled himself on the original Ripper. The pat-
tern of the killings, the way in which he set about
rearranging the victim's bodies, suggested he had
thought long and hard about what was to be his
lifetime's task.

It was as I was reading a book about the Ripper
—I had to peruse them at the library, Mummy
would have had a fit if I had brought one home!—
that an idea came into my head. And the more I
thought about it, the more daring and clever it
seemed. The main thought worrying me was that
the police must, in the course of their investigations, stop attributing Eileen's death to the Hammer: why, most of the details of the murder had
been different to previous Hammer ones. Under
pressure of publicity they had said it was his work:
but pure plodding police work would show it was a
brick that had cracked her skull, that her body had

not been rearranged in a particular way, and would lead to another conclusion. Unless— Unless something were to happen that would finally convince them it was the Hammer's work.

I got up early on the Saturday after the killing and told Mummy that I wouldn't be taking her, as I usually did, to the Horse and Hounds for a lunchtime drink. I had resolved to do some research for my next paper at the History Society. She was a little disappointed, but she always understood the importance of the History Society to me. I took the little cassette machine I used to record chamber music from its holder in the car; and I drove up the hill through Princetown. It was a glorious day, and I drove down to my favourite country spot, the field overlooking the brook. There was no sign of human habitation from there: you wouldn't believe that just over the brow of a hill two miles away lay the edge of a crowded urban conurbation.

I had brought some sandwiches and beer, and I spread out the little tartan rug I usually used when I came up here. I looked out at the dark yellows, greens, greys, and purples of the edge of the moor. The field I was in was pure green, and sheep picked at the grass lazily in a corner. Below, a stream prattled ceaselessly along on its shallow bed of stones. Although the day was cold and crisp, the sun, untouched by clouds, was warming. I had on a thick pullover, and felt wholly at ease.

After I had eaten, I went to the car to fetch a tape recorder. I placed it on the rug, and took out the little script I had written. I went over it once again, making corrections. The whole idea was so daring, I hardly had the courage to go through with it. But

I wasn't committed yet: I could make the recording, and then destroy it if it proved unsatisfactory. I put a handkerchief over the receiver and pulled my head down, speaking out of my throat, low and gruff, in the best Lancashire accent I could muster. It wasn't my natural accent: I had been educated at grammar school. But I had grown up with it all my life, and my imitation was deemed perfect by the members of the History Society, whom I used to entertain wittily in the pub we went to after our meetings. I would have to stop those imitations for a time. I tried my little speech out three or four times on the tape until it was perfect and there was no trace of my usual accent. My voice sounded deep and distorted in the little machine. It was too good not to be used.

I went back to the car, and carefully wiped the cassette clean of fingerprints with a cloth I had bought for the purpose. I put it into the envelope I had prepared, using gloves. I wrote the address out laboriously, in shaky capital letters, with my left hand. I would destroy the biro and the cloth afterwards. Then I drove off, in a great semicircle around the Farleigh conurbation, until I reached a part of town I didn't know. At the first postbox I found, I popped it in. There was no one around. Only after I had done the deed did a little thrill touch me: I had taken a terrible risk. My scheme would either work, and leave me in the clear for good, or lead them straight to me.

On Monday I extracted myself from the office early to go and buy an evening paper. The news was blazoned across the front pages: VOICE OF A MONSTER; HAMMER TAUNTS POLICE. I was chortling: I couldn't wait to get back to watch the television news of the press conference Inspector Prescott had held that morning. Mummy was surprised to see me so early; I told her that I had been taken ill with a slight stomachache. She was watching TV as usual, and I perched on the arm of the chair beside her. I was in a thoroughly good humour. She observed, "I'm glad you're so much better, dear. You seem to have quite forgotten that History Society business last week."

"Oh, that," I said dismissively, as the evening news came on; they had gone to town on it on the local programme: the full press conference was shown. Inspector Prescott sat behind a table with his modest little look. He was flanked by two burly police officers. "I want to play to you a tape that we received in this morning's post," he said, switching on a cassette player. My Lancashire tones drawled out, frozen in crude electric crackle, as unlike my voice as could be conceived.

"I thought I would send you a message, Victor, to help you. It's getting too easy for me. I've done nine now and you're no nearer getting me than you were on the first day. Right? I did her good and proper on Thursday night, didn't I? And a police car not a block away from where I was on the job. Isn't that bloody amazing? I don't know what it is you boys do all day. It all comes out of ratepayers' money. Anyway, she was a cinch to do."

There was a click, and I was momentarily puzzled. It was at the place where I had given details of what she was wearing, and the exact location of her injury. The aim was to show that the tape was not a hoax. Then I realised that the police were deliberately concealing such details from the public. The voice clicked back on: "Not doing very well, are we, Victor? Number nine. I do it in order to tease you, boss"—I couldn't resist using Jack the Ripper's taunt—"as much as for the women. That'll give your shrinks something to think about, won't it? You won't be able to stop number ten, because that's coming, and soon, and you still haven't the faintest idea who I am or where to find me. By-by." My voice had a mocking tone, as I clicked off.

Inspector Prescott said tersely, "That was the voice of a very sick man. We are certain that the tape is genuine, for a number of reasons we cannot disclose. I want to say three things, though, to the public. The first is that in sending us this tape, we have been provided with important clues as to the perpetrator of the series of murders that have affected the eastern quarter of Farleigh. Our investigations, which after months of painstaking effort were leading us inexorably towards the killer, have now been helped by a series of vital confirmatory clues, and I can assure you that this is a case that everyone in the West Midlands force is determined to clear up as soon as possible. Secondly, we remain convinced that the murderer is being shielded by someone—by a wife, a close relative, a friend. Once again we appeal to this person to come forward and provide us with confidential information at the earliest opportunity. This man is a danger to the public, and must be apprehended as soon as possible. However dear he may be to someone, he cannot be treated until this happens. Finally, I want any member of the public who has heard this voice, or believes he can recognise its author, to telephone

95823 as soon as possible. I'll repeat that: 95823.
Don't be afraid of coming forward. You will be interviewed in total confidence. Don't be afraid of
being thought a fool as we eliminate a suspect from
our enquiries. Out of the thousands of calls we expect to receive, one may lead us to the person we
are seeking. Now I'll play the tape again, and I
want you to think—think hard—about whether it
reminds you of anyone."

I did, and as the dead, unruffled Lancashire tones
spilled out, I admired my handiwork. It certainly
didn't sound like me.

My mother changed channels halfway through.
"I can't bear to hear him, dear. He sounds so awful.
And so complacent about it all. Ugh, it makes me
shudder."

I quickly settled back into my old way of life: the
office routine, carrying out old Palmer's dictates,
keeping the secretaries to their work, and the endless chitchat with my mother in the evenings and
at weekends. I made a point of not omitting to take
her to the Horse and Hounds, her favourite Saturday pub, for the next few weekends. Life resumed
its steady, measured stride, and I felt no twinge of
temptation to get involved again in the vice which
had nearly led to my downfall. I had been a little
bored before, a little unsatisfied at the way life
seemed to have settled into a rut, had failed to de-
velop. But now I realised how precarious was the
comfort of my settled ways, and how precious to
me. I didn't want to tempt fate again. And I was
disgusted with myself, for yielding to temptation:
my close call had only been due punishment.

Yet one thing lingered: my fascination with the Hammer case, in which I had played a small, but important role. I scanned every article about it, and grew more and more amused at the way the police seemed almost perversely to misinterpret every scrap of evidence. From the saliva on the stamp on the envelope I had sent, they had decided that the Hammer belonged to a rare blood group: this contradicted one finding at the scene of an earlier crime, where blood other than that of the victim had been found. The police were now wondering whether the Hammer had in fact been responsible for the first murder. That the tape was authentic, and that the Hammer had been responsible for Eileen's death, they had no doubt at all. The police had been inundated by thousands of calls after the voice had been played, and had even installed a number which you could dial in order to listen to the voice again.

At the September committee meeting of the History Society, Eric Ballance, the history lecturer at the polytechnic, was in a dominating mood. Our president, Wilfred Boscawen, was a dear old gentleman who owned one of the few remaining Georgian houses in the town; we held our meetings there. Wilfred was president because of that.

He had peered benignly down the table and wondered if we had any suggestions for our summer programme. There were six of us there—I had to admit interest had been declining recently. I held back, for fear of seeming too forward. Eric, a rugged outdoor type, with hair over his collar and a rather slack habit, I thought, for someone in his

position, of not wearing a tie, leaned forward. "I'd
like to propose a rather ambitious project. That we
examine the way in which the dominant class of
the town has evolved over the last fifty years. It
seems to me this would be a very constructive
study in socio-historical exploration, and one
which if done successfully could be published as a
paper which might attract national attention and
dissemination.

"Let me explain: in my view there has been a
very considerable evolution in the socioeconomic
makeup of the dominating class in Farleigh. From
being a town with a long established social structure, dominated by the leading professional class—
who, it might be said, evolved ties of marriage with
the old gentry class that owned the land around the
town—Farleigh changed: the dominant class was
compelled against its better instincts to open up,
for it was challenged by the new industrial wealth
that emerged in the latter half of the nineteenth
century. These men came of humble origins, and
were not initially allowed into the privileged circle
that ran the town; but their wealth, after a generation, became irresistible to professional families
seeking to marry off younger daughters, and the
two groups gradually became integrated into one.
Then, secondly, a new shopkeeper class brought up
in the wake of the town's expansion and industrial
development moved in and itself sought to break
into the elite, copying their manners and behaviour
and pretensions and so on. However, this class
lacked the wealth with which the industrialists had
endowed the old ruling class, so it was forced into a

position of subordination once held by the new industrial class itself. . . ."

I wondered how this was going down with Boscawen, a real gentleman, one of the last of what Eric would have defined as "the professional class." Actually the old boy, by dint of a marriage his father had made to a prosperous landowner, probably regarded himself as "gentry." I pinched myself. I was beginning to think in Eric's terms. He was droning on in his heavy sociological way. Wilfred wore a glazed expression, as though he had nodded off, although I didn't believe he had. A couple of the others certainly had.

Eric looked up, realised that his audience's attention was wandering, and raised his voice. "What I propose is this. My students are skilled in conducting oral history interviews; if they could gather material in the form of a multiplicity of interviews, I would be happy to work through the material, analyse the socioeconomic changes in the town, and present my findings to the History Society. I am sure such a paper would earn a great deal more attention that the somewhat academic and, if I may say so, esoteric studies and papers than have been delivered to the society in the past. I would imagine that such a paper would arouse the attention of the local news media—even television perhaps."

"Yes, well," said Wilfred, clearing his throat. "I'm not too sure that it wouldn't all be rather a bore. Are there no other subjects the society would care to pursue?"

Eric gritted his teeth. "We have our next meeting on May 8 and no speaker has yet been found; has

anyone a better idea?" The others shifted uneasily.
This was my cue. I came in smugly. "I have a pro-
posal, and one that I feel would arouse more interest than anything suggested so far." Eric glared at
me. I outlined my idea of a paper concerning the
similarities between the Ripper and Hammer cases.
"What a splendid idea," said Wilfred at the end.
"A good, old-fashioned Victorian melodrama. How
extraordinarily interesting. I must say I had seen
something about these horrid crimes in the newspaper."

The other members of the committee all looked
relieved at the suggestion, and without discussion
we agreed to go ahead on the project.

Afterwards Eric came up to me with a smile. "I
must say I didn't reckon you had it in you to dream
up a subject as sexy as that. I've got to hand it to
you."

"I beg your pardon," I said stiffly. "My paper
will be strictly of historical interest, and will not
cater to anyone's prurience."

"Forget it," he said with a smile.

I spent the next three weeks absorbed in the subject. I had no time for anything else. One day, after
I had returned from work and was busily researching in a corner of the room while the television
clattered on, I noticed that Mummy had slipped
out of her chair and was on the ground, trying
rather feebly to pick herself up. The noise from the
set had drowned out the noise of her fall. I rushed
forward and gently lifted her back up. "That's all
right," she said in her frail way. "I was trying to
get up. I have to go next door."

"Well, here, let me help you," I said. "You silly Mummy. You should have called out."

"I didn't want to disturb you in your work."

"It's not work," I chided gently. "It's my hobby. You don't have to regard it as sacrosanct. You know you're what I really care about in the world."

She smiled her sweet smile up at me. "Is that really so, darling?"

"Of course. You know it is." She walked a little more steadily to the bathroom, hardly needing my assistance at the end. And she came back to her chair afterwards unaided, and got cross when I offered to help her to bed.

But afterwards, I took my usual glass of port before retiring. I sat down and considered. She was getting older, and had been doing so much faster recently. She was frailer and less assertive. Was it because I hadn't been paying her much attention? Did she feel that I was losing interest in her, was that the significance of her last remark? Or was it just age? She was seventy-seven now, and really beginning to be at an age when one had to be careful. I resolved to pay her more attention: the biggest worry was of something like a fall which might break her hip and render her unable to walk. With me at the office she would be bedridden, or at least confined to her chair all day, and that wouldn't do at all. She cherished her independence, even if now it consisted only in wandering from one room to another. I resolved that I would work only when her attention was taken up by television.

My fear that I was in some way growing careless of others seemed echoed at the office, where I found that my new self-confidence, instead of meeting with old Palmer's approval, actually irritated him. I remember on one occasion we were discussing whether to set up a link with a professional chartered surveying firm, as so many of our clients now required full structural surveys and we weren't in a position to do them. Old Palmer argued against the idea. "This company does very well keeping to the things it knows about, and that is buying and selling properties."

His son chipped in. "But, honestly, I think it'd be useful to be able to refer clients directly to a surveyor we approved of. Almost all buyers want a survey done now."

For once I added my voice to the opposition. "The trouble is that clients ask us whom we recommend as a surveyor, and on an informal basis we always end up telling them to go to Rutherfords. If we had a formal arrangement, we would at least get something for our pains, instead of acting as an advertising agency for them."

Old Palmer's voice was unexpectedly hard. "Then we, not Rutherfords, will be held responsible if things go wrong with the structure of the house. I don't want to get involved in a company that cannot be relied upon to maintain our own standards of excellence." He said it with such finality that we dropped the subject. But I noticed that he didn't bid me his customary—his invariable—good night on leaving the office, and for three days hardly spoke to me. After that he eased up. But I resolved to be careful. He was the partner with the financial share in the company, and I could not afford to be too self-assured.

The great day approached. I had finished the paper more than ten days before, writing and rewriting it so that it would both read and declaim well. It was my first paper for the society for more than four years, and I put everything I had into it, stylistically and historically. The research was thorough; the footnotes comprehensive. I practiced reading it dozens of times, to see that my delivery and flow were perfect. It was thirty-two pages long and the first few times I read it, I found myself drying up halfway through. I decided that I had to take it more slowly, at a more measured pace, and that a jug of water, as well as a lectern, were essential. I would arrange this myself, as I was responsible for the setting up of the room.

I arrived early in Wilfred's drawing room, to arrange the chairs. It was a lovely old house, with a fine Georgian frontage, one of the three such left in the high street, which now rather discordantly boasted a Wimpeys and a Tescos, among other landmarks of our modern civilisation. The front rooms were rarely used, perhaps because they looked out upon those depressing shops, or perhaps because Wilfred had no use for them. The old boy preferred to live in a small, comfortable room he had at the back of the house with a deep wide armchair and footrest, where he sucked his pipe and read his books and dozed in peace. He had never married and, apart from elderly parents who had died years before, lived on his own. A housekeeper came in every day and did for him. I suppose I rather got on with him because he was an elderly bachelor who had come to terms with a restricted existence, like me. And he was a gentleman of the old school. They didn't make them like that any more.

We put out fifty chairs. Even that was inadequate for the crowd that did show up. Usually around twenty people came faithfully and regularly, bringing about half a dozen guests. Our total membership was around sixty, and every member was allowed to bring one guest. That night ninety-six people crowded in: I counted them all. There weren't enough chairs to go round, so some people sat on the floor and some stood at the back. I had my heart in my mouth as Wilfred introduced me. At the back I could see Eric with a rueful grin.

I had decided to make the talk as exciting as possible, while expunging all the squalid details that I had come across in my research into the Ripper's killings. They would only have fallen flat on such an audience, and my purpose was more serious. I wanted to do two things: to show that the Hammer had carefully modelled himself on the Ripper's methods, and so must be a literate man with some interest in history; and to show how the killings affected the way of life of a whole community. My theory on the second score was that his contemporaries had reacted in exactly the same way we were: the popular press had generated widespread hysteria, the police had set hundreds of people to work on the case, and no one in the end was caught; the original Ripper was never apprehended. The same seemed likely to be true of the Hammer case—although it remained to be seen whether the killings would tail off, as in the Ripper case.

The talk took me the best part of an hour to deliver. I started well, then got a little hoarse halfway through, and it took a minute or two to recover. I was thankful when I reached the end. The applause sounded loud enough. We had a little break, for which I was grateful, before questions, which were all rather easy. I was beginning to enjoy myself when the meeting came to an end. When I stepped back from the little lectern, Wilfred congratulated me: "That was absolutely excellent. Absolutely first-class, old boy." He gave my arm a squeeze, a rare measure of approval for him. "Let me offer you a drink before you go off for the serious business of the evening." It was our custom after History Society meetings to go to the Pakenham Arms, the only pub in town with a semblance of gentility, to down a few drinks there. It was unheard of for Wilfred to offer me one.

As I turned to follow him to his room, a number of members of the society came up. "Very, very good," said one. "First-rate," said another.

I told them that I would follow them down to the pub.

My gaze froze for a minute. Beyond them, making his way towards me, was Inspector Prescott, accompanied by a youngish man in an open-necked shirt who looked vaguely familiar. The alarm must have shown on my face; it took seconds to recover myself, I was so taken aback.

He looked at me apologetically—or was it with a slightly ironical smile? I couldn't believe the man was capable of irony. "I just wanted to say how very much I enjoyed your talk, sir," he said, proferring his hand. "It's given me plenty to think about."

"In what respect?" I asked nervously.

"Oh, I can't afford not to follow everything up. The thoroughness of your research has given me some valuable insights into the mind of our friend. In fact, I wonder if you might at some stage make a copy of the paper available to me. It's a help just to be able to justify your point about the historical similarity of the two cases. If our man is a fairly well-read type, well, it narrows the field."

So that was all. I looked with some contempt at the thin, serious, middle-aged man in front of me, slightly tawdrily dressed, the tie at an angle. The poor police were still so absolutely clueless that they had come to my talk to try and pick up a lead. I was almost angry with the little man—he had no right to come to a respectable gathering like this, to arouse the curiousity of my fellow members as to how he knew a respectable man like myself. But I reassured myself: people would think I had met him merely in the course of researching my talk. I said a little coldly, "I'm glad I can be of some help. Anything that can be done to speed up the arrest of this monster is to be encouraged."

"You can say that again, sir. I just hope you're wrong about the eventual outcome of the case. We aim to get our man. And we're closer than you might think."

I raised my eyebrows politely. "I certainly hope so." We exchanged smiles and he followed the departing crowd.

The man in the open-necked shirt introduced himself. "I'm John Jones, presenter of BBC Midlands' regional news programme." He acted as though I knew exactly who he was; the face was indeed vaguely familiar—the face one saw before switching to another channel. "I found your talk very interesting; very interesting indeed. I wondered if you would be prepared to expand on a couple of points you made, on my programme. Just a short thing. A five-minute spot. As you must be aware, there is great public interest in the Hammer story."

I looked a little stuffily at him. "I can't say I've ever appeared on television before. I'm not sure it would be appropriate—"

"Nothing to worry about," he said. "Most people we interview have never appeared on the box. It's just a question of repeating one or two of the things you've said here today. I'm sure they'd be of general interest." He took my hesitation for assent. "Good. I wonder whether you could come to the studio tomorrow morning, so we could run it on our afternoon programme?"

"That wouldn't do," I said flatly. "I work in the morning."

"I'm sure they'll understand, just this once. Your boss will want to watch you on the box." I wasn't sure he would. But it occurred to me that if any of the others were to get an opportunity like this, I was sure that old Palmer and myself would be understanding. And then I reflected that Mummy would see me too, and have the thrill of her life. She loved television and worshipped the people that appeared on it. Just imagine if my face materialised on the screen in front of her. It'd give her a lift, and she hadn't been so very well lately. . . .

"Very well," I said, and took down the details. The others had all left by now. Wilfred led me into his cosy little room, and offered me a glass of malt whisky, which I gratefully took. I luxuriated in the soothing of my first-night nerves. I had never gone through anything like that before. Wilfred said, "Well done again. Most interesting. A great deal more so than that frightful man Ballance's spoken history, or whatever he calls it. A lot of dreadful old pensioners making things up for the sake of being in front of a microphone."

"I'm sure it has its value," I said patronisingly.

"I believe he had ambitions to become secretary of the Society. Asked me about it, in fact. I told him that I didn't think there was any question of a vacancy," said Wilfred airily. "I was right, wasn't I?"

"Certainly," I said shortly. I sipped more of my drink. I was beginning to feel quite mellow. I always enjoyed a drink or two. But drinking with something to celebrate gave one a warm, comfortable feeling.

"Glad to hear it," said Wilfred. "Quite honestly, I'm beginning to get a little fed up with people like Ballance. Television society people, I call them. They've been brought up in the television age. I don't have one myself, by the way."

"Very sensible," I murmured.

"All those trendy sociologists' ideas. They want to mould society their own way. It's bad enough the way it's gone already. Take this town—the way it's changed for example. They built the Wimpey in a house that used to be owned by the Swindales. Of course it was their damn fault for ever selling the place."

I knew all about it. Palmer and Palmer had been the agents for the sale. And a very profitable one it

had been, too. I changed the subject. I had decided
to get away as soon as was decently possible to join
my friends, who would already be drinking in the
back room of the Pakenham. It was the one really
decent hostelry in town, where the wrong sort of
person didn't go. I was terribly afraid they would
leave before I got there. "I suppose you'll always
stay here?"

"Certainly." He looked at me suspiciously. "Oh,
of course. You're an estate agent. Well, I'm too involved to move. And I love this house. If I move,"
he said, with a twinkle in his eye, "it'd be taken
over by some frightful fast-food place; I've got to
keep up the standards of the town." He leaned forward unexpectedly. "Tell me. What was it that first
made you so interested in the Hammer?"

I looked at him complacently. "Why, it just
struck me as rather a good subject. Don't you think
so? Ideal. It's local, and the historical connection
made it irresistible."

His face expressed distaste. "It's an unattractive
subject, all the same. I thought you glossed over the
more gruesome bits very well. But while people are
still dying—it's rather tasteless. I hope you don't
mind my saying so," he added, suddenly worried
that he had offended me.

"Not in the least. I wondered about that myself.
But it's a subject of legitimate historical study, provided it's dealt with in the spirit I hope I did. I
thought I did it without causing offence."

"Yes, I suppose so," he said morosely. "I hope
you don't mind me saying so," he said again. "But
you're the last person I would expect to get involved in a subject like this. I mean, what was your

last talk about? A discourse on the origin of the
names of the main streets in Farleigh, as I remember it."

"Something rather like that," I said. I was getting a little tired of the conversation. It seemed to
me that he was rambling on, saying every first
thought that came into his head. "I suppose I'm
interested in anything that affects the town I live
in. And these murders will long be a part of its
history."

"I don't see what you see in this place. Most of
it's an industrial slum now, and the town centre's
been ruined."

I looked at my watch. "Oh dear. Twenty past
ten. I know they'll be expecting me down at the
Pakenham. It really was very kind of you, Wilfred."

Outside I felt the fresh air on my face with relief.
I gave the house—the fine Georgian windows and
its upper-middle-class sobriety so defiant in the
face of the rather tatty shopfronts—a backward
glance. The old man was living in another century,
but I couldn't help feeling he had been getting at
me in some way. I was the more disturbed, because
until then I had only known the rather mean, mel-
ancholy, private side of the man and had admired
him. His old-world courtliness, it seemed, was on
the surface only. I was disappointed to discover
that we were all much the same underneath, whatever background we came from. As were murderers.

The dreary yellow streetlights illuminated my
path down the main street towards the Pakenham,
which was off a turning to the right. A police car

was parked further down the street, with its lights off, but I could see there were two occupants. What a fatuous place to wait for the Hammer, I thought rather tipsily. The lit-up sign of the pub's coat of arms was rather welcoming because there was no one about in the streets at all. Inside, in the back room, my crowd was making an abominable noise.

There were twelve of them; four I had never set eyes on before. Those I knew were Eric Ballance, who was rather subdued, I thought; Harry Blomfeld, a local solicitor; Edward Jones, who ran the local supermarket franchise; two friends of his from a firm of chartered accountants, Edward and John Williams; the town's main undertaker, Jacob Stewart; Roy Kennedy, who ran an off-licence; and the only one among them that wasn't middle-aged, Ernest Jones, Edward's son, a rather serious, studious type who seemed to enjoy the company of older men. The gathering was an important one for many of them; like me, I suspected that their social lives were confined only to their wives, the occasional dinner party with another couple, or the pub.

Blomfeld was holding forth, telling them the latest legal gossip. If anyone wanted to find out what was likely to be the result of any court case in that town over the next three weeks, they should come to the Pakenham on a night after a history society meeting. He stopped talking when he saw me. He was paunchy, with a round, jolly face and eyebrows that seemed contoured to the circularity of his flesh. "Oh, it's Cicero himself!" he said heartily. "We didn't think we'd have the pleasure of your company this evening. I think we all deserve a round for staying awake."

I knew I was in for it. I got them all a drink, them and their four guests. The publican, a tall, white-haired, distinguished-looking, rather stout man recognised me and was amiability itself. "Your crowd's put back a fair lot tonight," he said.

"Ah well, it's thirsty work listening to me," I replied. I bought myself a large vintage port, and settled down to enjoying its soothing, rather bookish heaviness. The four were guests of members, two from out of town. One man was a rather quiet fellow of about forty, with a large, heavy face and the big, bony hands, which he continually clasped and unclasped, of a farmer. It turned out that he worked in a bank. The other was a small, youngish man in his early thirties with an ingratiating grin, who seemed eager to please. He worked in industry —in a chemical plant; I could imagine him in charge of some laboratory. Both those guests worked in town; I wasn't interested in the others, who didn't.

"But Harry," interjected young Jones. "You've never been involved in a murder case. You can't know what a murderer is like." They were talking about the Hammer. I was pulled out of my contemplation of the people present, which was my favourite pastime.

"You're wrong there. When I was learning my articles, I was asked to help out on some of the paperwork and preparation for the Maudsley case." Maudsley was a homosexual, who had been jailed for the horrific killing of a number of young men a few years before; even I had heard of him, long before I became interested in such subjects. "I was present at a number of interviews on the case, and also watched him in court. He was an extraordinary chap, I can tell you.

"I still remember his rather grave, haggard appearance; the stony, steady, cool blue eyes, utterly cruel behind the thick spectacles. Talking to him, he gave the impression of being selfish and immensely intelligent. He knew exactly what he was doing, there was no obtuseness or confusion about his thoughts at all. He spoke in a quiet, very level way, like a scientist, detailing the full horror of his acts. He didn't seem to have any human feelings at all: it was as though his victims were of no consequence. What I couldn't understand about the man, was his detachment: how did he have the feelings inside that made him kill? Yet he must have had them, or he wouldn't have done so. I mean, his was the kind of mind that would take pleasure in crosswords and mathematical puzzles, not hurting people or indulging in sex, however perverse."

"Well," said Jones, in his dry way, "I should think he just bottled up his emotions. He was obviously a raving queer inside."

"No, that wasn't it. He seemed just to take pleasure in killing for its own sake. It was as though he was analysing the reactions of his victims, and the art of killing—if you could call it that—was of academic interest to him. Not unlike one of those Nazi doctors during the war. I don't believe he got pleasure out of it, not what you and I would call pleasure."

"Nonsense," cried Kennedy, who was rather a loud type. "He got all he could out of his victims.

That much was in the papers. It's just the same as everyone else—except bloody bent. Beyond belief." he added unnecessarily.

"What does the great historian of murderers think?" asked Jones a little mockingly.

I coughed deferentially. "I wouldn't think myself qualified to comment on his lusts, as all of you do," I said. That raised a laugh. "What I think is most interesting is why he repeats his murders. Why he has a stylised way of killing. I think the real pleasure he gets is from the publicity, and from taunting the police to show they can't catch him. The killings themselves, well, they may stem from gratification or they may reflect the fact that he has no feelings. But he certainly gets a feeling of accomplishment from the whole grisly business: from preparing the murder, carrying it out, carrying out the sadistic practices afterwards, then watching the police make fools of themselves."

"I'm sure that's right," said young Jones suddenly, with an intensity that for a moment left an embarrassed silence in its wake. "I mean," he said hastily, "I mean, he wouldn't go to all that trouble sending a tape to the police unless he enjoyed that bit of it."

Eric leaned forward. "It was an extraordinary tape. Extraordinary. So banal and boring in its message, yet so chilling. Absolutely to the point in all its formulations."

"Unlike the tapes you keep making," I couldn't resist putting in. "Must be a job getting old-age pensioners to stop going on about things." They all chuckled.

Eric smiled good-naturedly. "The tape bloody

well reminded me of your Lancashire imitation. You know, it was the first thing I thought of when I heard it. A little deeper, that's all; more nasal. But it sounded just like you. Do your Lancashire voice. Go on, do it," he said.

I reddened. The others looked at me expectantly. It would be stranger to refuse than not to: most evenings I put on a show. But to be linked to that tape—I couldn't believe Eric suspected anything. We cordially detested each other, but he was just having a joke at my expense. I made my voice slightly higher and as different from the tape as possible. "There's only one thing better than Liverpool and that's Merseyside." They all laughed.

"Deeper. You usually do it deeper."

I tried it a tone deeper. I felt a panic begin to rise within me. They were all staring at me, concentrating now, and it seemed that in their faces there was no longer laughter, but hostility and fear. Their eyes seemed to be drilling into me. I faltered, and then the moment was past, and I continued. When I had finished they clapped lightheartedly. "Remarkable," said Eric, "absolutely remarkable. You'll get a part, if they ever make a film about the murders."

"I think we ought to turn him into the police now," said the ingratiating newcomer in a soft voice. I glared at him: I had hardly met him.

"No, he won't do, he's too small and tubby," said Blomfeld. "Remember, about the only thing that's certain about the Hammer is that he's tall and strong, so that he can sneak up on his victims and give them their tap on the head. There's never a sign of a struggle, which suggests he's pretty overpowering, not someone his victims can get away from."

"Either that, or they trust him. He may be very attractive to women," put in old man Jones.

"That rules out Harry once and for all," said Eric to general amusement.

"He's got to know how to handle a tape recorder," I said, recovering my spirits and looking pointedly at Eric. "Eric fits the bill. And he's well built."

"No. Any woman'd run a mile if they saw him coming," put in Jones, to a whoop of laughter.

"Steady, young man, steady. I've not done so badly in my time," said Eric through gritted teeth, stubbing out a cigarette in the ash tray. We were bought another round by Blomfeld.

"So what's the sociological background of the Hammer?" I asked, turning the questioning towards Eric. "Go on, you should be able to deduce that."

"My methods of investigation are empirical and evidence-based. I don't make guesses from insufficient evidence, as so many so-called historians do," he retorted. "However, if you asked me to hazard a non-historical guess, I'd say our man belonged to socioeconomic class D. He's a reasonably well-read and literate man, as Harry has established, certainly not a manual worker, and yet obviously good with his hands, who can wield an instrument like an industrial hammer with expertise. I wouldn't think he was much above that sort of class because prostitutes are traditionally the release of men like that, who can't afford girlfriends or mistresses and who don't mix in the social circles where they might have access to other women. If he is married, it's to some frowsy type, who'll try to keep him anchored to house and home."

"You'd not say that's the only type of person who consorts with prostitutes?" said Blomfeld. "Why—" He checked himself. "I'm damn sure a few of my clients from pretty good backgrounds do. Frowsy—as you call them—wives aren't confined to the working classes, you know."

"Maybe not," said Eric, a little uncertainly.

"I find it incredible," I interrupted petulantly, "that anyone still believes that happily married men, as a matter of course, go to bed with the women in their social circle."

Eric was about to say something, but checked himself. He was suddenly aware of how traditional a society Farleigh still was. Our circle did not come from the kind of wife-swapping university and tech society he came from, with its modern morality—if you could call it that—and live-together couples. This was a settled society, with values and respect for relationships, of the kind that had kept Britain going for generations. I wondered whether even such an insensitively self-assertive man as Eric felt that there was something missing at his stage in life, and whether that was why he had joined the society, to enjoy a thoroughly old-fashioned kind of companionship among moral people. Only now was he realising how big the gap between his values and ours was.

And then a pang of conscience struck me. It occurred to me that I was the only one present—who had consorted with a prostitute. But then I had an excuse: I wasn't even married, and had no outlet at all for those sorts of feelings. And I had fallen only once. Anyway, it was all in the past.

Our little circle broke good-humouredly after two more rounds, and an hour and a half after the landlord had called time. He was always generous to us, as good customers, and he kept an orderly house; the police didn't bother him. My car was parked down on the high street, and I wondered if I'd had too much to drink. But I'd never been stopped in my life, and the house was only five minutes away by car. I turned out of the side street into the main street, after wishing everyone good night. I walked a few yards and then came to a dead stop. In front of me was a red Cortina with a distinctive number plate. At least I remembered the letters, not the number: WET 834 S. WET: it had stood out at me like a reproof that sodden night as I had emerged from the building site, past the two cars between me and the unoccupied police car. Surely there couldn't be two red Cortinas with the number WET? ET was not, after all, the town's identifying mark, which was US. And the car was here. . . .

Just chance, just coincidence. I must play down these false alarms, or I would end up a nervous wreck. I walked on. In that instant I was sure there was someone behind me, and the state of my nerves was such that I turned to have a look. There was nothing: just a couple of engines interrupting the stillness as my friends drove off. I was alone, and that was none too reassuring. I walked on, hurriedly, towards the side street where the car was parked. I heard a car start up behind me, and a little way away, the Cortina's headlights came on, dipped, and the car swung round, doing a sharp U-turn in the road. The street lighting was too dim to catch a glimpse of who was inside. . . .

And then I was certain he had been there, he had been attending our intimate little gathering. Why else had he slunk out of sight when I had turned, except to avoid recognition? It was someone I knew personally that owned that car, and the thought sickened me. Because the only reason for secrecy was that he had witnessed something on that dreadful night, and he knew that I had recognised the car. So there had been a witness, and a witness who knew who I was, and a witness who was one of my acquaintances. I felt the familiar weakening in the legs, and stumbled into my car. It had soured the triumph of the evening.

In the morning, I was committed to my television appearance. I hadn't slept that night, and woke up a great deal, sweating. I had hardly exchanged two words with my mother when she asked me how the talk had gone. From this I think she must have assumed it went badly, and had probably worried about me all night. I had been brusque, and felt guilty, but would have time to apologise to her that evening.

Meanwhile, I badly wanted to wriggle out of the television programme. But that would have been suspicious in itself. I was beginning to be sick of the whole Hammer thing. What had possessed me to take an interest in it, after the terrible thing that had happened? I kept asking myself. Just the fact that something had happened to me, for once, that elevated me above the ordinary run of things. But it was dangerous to play with fire, and I resolved that once the television programme was over I would have nothing more to do with it. I rang old Palmer.

To my surprise, he was a little tetchy. "Oh dear," was his reaction. "We've got quite a work load on this morning. I can't have people coming in and going out whenever they feel like it."

"This will have been my only morning off in fourteen years," I reminded him. "And it's something special. It's not every day one gets to appear on television."

Mummy, instead was ecstatic. "I don't believe it! I'll see you on my screen, right here, in the morning room! I'm going to ring up everyone I know, even Jack!" Jack was her younger brother, who never came to see us, but always sent a Christmas card.

"Mummy, honestly, it's nothing, really." She had forgotten all about my sullen mood of the night before.

The television company sent a car to pick me up after I had had my usual breakfast of a pot of tea and two marmalade-laden chunks of bread. I always ate a lot at that time because I was hungry on getting up, and because I usually had nothing more than a sandwich at lunch.

I felt very grand, sitting in the back of the Austin Princess, gazing out at the landmarks of everyday life, sweeping down the dual carriageway, past the old crematorium, past the building site where . . .

The car stopped outside the television studio, which was in a large modern building in the nearby town of Ironport. I was taken upstairs in a

lift by a girl with a smile as wide as her face, and
the two top buttons of her blouse undone. No one
seemed to wear a tie in the place, which was very
relaxed and informal. A touch too much so for my
taste. I was taken into a room where John Jones
offered me a cup of coffee. He eased my nerves by
listing for me the questions they would ask. "It's
just an informal programme, so relax. We won't be
trying to pin you to the wall, as we would a politi-
cian." He grinned. "If you're ready, we're on in a
couple of minutes."

I was ushered into a small room where a rather
blowsy lady told me to sit in front of a mirror.
With practiced ease, she smeared powder all over
my face with a puff. I felt ridiculous, and the stuff
seemed to get in my eyes and nose. "Is this absolutely necessary?" I asked irritably.

"No, you can look like a corpse instead, dearie,"
she answered. Then, more kindly, she added: "Under the lights you'd look as white as a sheet unless
we put a bit of colour in your cheeks."

"I'm that pale, am I?"

"Everyone needs it." I was ushered into the studio: this consisted of a room with a long table and a
screen behind it; the presenter was already there.
When I sat down, the glare of lights was extraordinary: banks of white blazing orbs were aimed at
my face. I could hardly see beyond them to where
large cameras mounted on mobile trolleys moved
dimly backwards and forwards. At my side, suddenly I saw my face appear on a large television
screen; I was disconcerted, all the more so because
my unease showed up in giant form on the screen.

"Take no notice," said John. "Try to speak to me,

not looking directly into the camera. It looks unnatural otherwise." It was all very well him saying
so, but I was always curious to see what I looked
like on the screen, and every time I looked I felt
absurd. It was most off-putting.

"Thirty seconds to go." I noticed the presenter
seemed as tense as I was. I sipped from the glass on
the table. A green light suddenly turned to red and
almost as suddenly he turned to me, his face practiced and professional with ease. "Harry Denman,
you've made a special study of The Hammer Horror case, establishing pretty conclusively that the
killer must have consciously modelled himself on
the acts of Jack the Ripper in the last century.
What is it that makes you so certain?"

I had to summarise the contents of my rather
long and complex argument in less than a minute. I
was close to getting to the main point when I was
cut off with another question. "So what you're saying is that the Hammer must be a literate and intelligent man? What do you think, then, drives him to
the acts he commits?"

I wasn't saying that, or at least, I hadn't got close
to saying it, and I had no qualifications at all to
discuss the forces that drove him. I hesitated. "I
really can't say. But if you look at the historical
parallel, what drove the Ripper was, ultimately, a
fear of women, something stemming, I suppose,
from a rejection by women."

"That's very interesting. So you're suggesting
that the Hammer is not a happily married man?"

I really didn't know what I was talking about.
"Happily married, no; or rather, I doubt it. But he

may be married. A lot of married men don't get on with their wives," I said with a wan smile.

He smiled back mildly. "Absolutely. Can I ask, Mr. Denman, just what it was that first interested you in the Hammer case. I understand you are an estate agent by profession? I understand you were at some stage interviewed by the police in connection with one case."

I tensed slightly, but rose to the occasion. "I am the secretary of the Farleigh History Society and a subject like that, with its obvious historical connotations, is very much within our purlieu."

"That's all we have time for, I'm afraid," he said, taking advantage of the pause in my answer. "Well, from the unsolved Hammer case to a case involving a solution, or more precisely, a solvent. Fifteen-year-old Wayne Ingrams was found dead on Tuesday, in what appears to have been a case of death by solvent abuse—more commonly known as glue-sniffing. This case has highlighted . . ."

I was whisked out. They said they would be sending a cheque to my address. I found myself once more in the back seat of the car, being driven off in a squeal of tyres. Now that I had a moment to myself, I told the driver to take me straight to my office, not the house. He radioed back for instructions, and then did as I told him.

I felt rather grand as the car left me on the pavement. I could see Diane, the typist young Paul was sweet on, eyeing me. "Well look who's here," she said loudly, as I came in. "The TV star himself. How did it go? When will you be on?"

"I'm on the seven o'clock programme. It was all right."

"You're all ponced up," said young Palmer cheekily. I remembered my makeup, which they hadn't taken off.

"Oh, that," I said in embarrassment. "Thank you for reminding me."

Old Palmer looked at me stonily from his large desk at the end of the office. "When you've finished, can you step by a moment? It's about Number 12 Green Street."

"What, that hasn't fallen through again?" I exclaimed incredulously.

"That bloody Simpson woman's pulled out. She says it's got to be two thousand lower."

"But she's already accepted. . . ."

The routine of the office went on.

At home I joined my mother to watch the programme. I helped myself to a dry sherry, gave her her usual whisky, and settled onto the comfortable chair beside her. I was anxious before it started. But I need not have worried. I thought I looked rather flushed. But my answers seemed firmly stated and I had a certain natural *gravitas* and authority. Or so I thought. After it was over, my mother turned to me. "You wonderful boy. That was excellent. I can hardly believe it was you." We had a celebratory drink.

At length she said, "What did they mean by your special knowledge of one case?"

She never missed a thing. I said hurriedly, "That was the particular case I devoted most of my research to. I couldn't have investigated them all."

That satisfied her. "It is all a nasty business—but

very interesting," she added, in case she had offended me.

I was seething. I knew it must have been that bloody Inspector Prescott who had told the presenter. I wanted to ring him up and tell him what I thought of him: all the inquiries were supposed to be confidential. But I remembered the pledge I had made, to finish with this bloody case once and for all. As far as I was concerned the Hammer affair was over. That was an iron decision, and I would stick to it. With luck the whole fuss would now blow over. As for the witness in the car—perhaps it had been coincidence, perhaps there indeed were two cars with the same number plate. But that didn't explain his hiding from me. I shrugged. It was over. Back to normal life.

Three days later I was not giving a thought to the Hammer business. It had receded into my unconscious. I closed the front door, went down the short path to the garden gate, and went to my car, which was parked a few yards away. The street contained only a pedestrian and two mothers chatting, while their children fidgeted. A movement—that was all —caught my eye: it was a figure, I was sure of it, skipping back into a side street, as though he had done so because he had seen me. I found myself wondering whether to take a look, then stopped myself. It was absurd of me to get upset and excited every time there was a small movement; I must get a hold of myself, expunge this Hammer business entirely from my system. With an effort I got into the car and drove to work. Nothing further happened—or seemed to happen. That day.

Or the next, or the next. On the Friday, I left the
office a little later than usual, at half past six, because I liked to see that the outstanding work had
been seen to before the weekend. The others had
left at five-thirty. The street was very empty when
I switched off the lights, but darkness would not
fall for another hour. It had been a tiresome day,
with rain spitting down more on than off, and I felt
a little tired and in need of rest. I decided I
wouldn't drive straight home: the flat was getting a
little claustrophobic now that Mummy refused to
budge out of her chair much, and I thought I
would take an evening paper, take a stroll, and have
a drink. There was a towpath I knew down by the
canal which took one to a pleasant pub nearby, by a
bridge, where one could sit out if it was warm
enough. I walked down the few streets that led to it
and soon found myself on well-trodden earth underneath. I felt a little refreshed by the breeze by
the canal, and even didn't mind the light patter on
my face. I wondered if I wasn't after all, a country
type. Perhaps I would retire at some stage on the
small savings I had built up to a cottage where I
could live cheaply and comfortably, without working. I would miss work, though. And then I remembered that I could only do that when Mummy
wasn't there anymore, and that didn't bear thinking about.

I paused, just short of the pub, gazing out over
the still water of the canal at a big black warehouse
up from a green bank. There was something restful
about the patter of raindrops on water. Behind the
pub, the bridge crouched gracefully. It wasn't a
beautiful scene, but somehow I enjoyed the compo-

sition of that low bridge, the dark building, and the straight canal. And then it happened again; as I approached the bridge, I noticed there was a man standing on it looking at me. He turned abruptly when I glanced up, and started walking quickly down off it, to the other side. I hesitated: was I imagining things again? Should I go after him, or forget it? In the end I did neither. I stayed there long enough for him to disappear into the buildings on the other side, then rather slowly walked to the top of the bridge looking for him. Of course he had gone. Cursing my indecisiveness, I walked back to the pub and ordered a pint.

It was only as I was ordering the second that a thought occurred to me: perhaps he had seen me go into the pub; perhaps he would be waiting outside now. For heaven's sake, I told myself unconvincingly, you're imagining the whole thing. Who would want to spy on me? My first thought was the police, whose suspicions could have been aroused again. But would they be so clumsy in allowing themselves to be spotted? And what good would it do them to keep an occasional eye on me—unless, in their opinion, to prevent another murder? Well, they would get no satisfaction on that score. Who else was there, but the mystery driver of the red Ford Cortina? A witness to my crime. Again, though, what good would come from his observing me? Much simpler for him to have gone straight to the police, or to blackmail me. Neither had happened since his first sighting. Why just watch me?

Anyway, while I was pondering in the pub, time was getting on, and the light had been failing outside. I thought of the walk home with sudden unease. I had a slug of whisky to give me courage and left, looking carefully from side to side. There was no one on the towpath. It was a lonely walk, in the night by the deserted canal, and I couldn't rid myself of the sensation that I was being watched. I walked quite quickly, unlike my usual self when I was feeling relaxed. I felt more insecure still as I walked into the shadow of the protective buildings leading up towards the centre of town. The buildings were deserted warehouses too, with rubble and large old dustbins between them. I had never noticed how empty the area was.

A scuffling noise set my nerves on edge. It was a cat sliding out of a doorway. I looked behind, but it was too dark to see down to the water's edge now. There was no one in the alley, but I was sure I was being watched. How could that be? It wasn't logical. I had to get a grip on myself, not let myself panic like this. All the same, if I was being followed it was better to run. Damme, I thought, it wasn't. If he was looking for a sign to betray my fear, that would be the sign. Anyway, I wasn't being followed.

I reached the main road with a gasp of relief. There were a few people about. As I hurried along, I kept looking round, to the alley entrance. But no one came out. My fears had been groundless. So the watcher on the bridge hadn't waited for me after all. Perhaps he hadn't been watching me at all; perhaps it had just been my imagination.

I had shopping to do on the way back; it was Wednesday, so the shops were open late: it was a convenient day to get the mid-week provisions. I went on to the Kwiksave. Beastly place, full of peo-

ple pushing trollies all over one's feet, and blue-
coated shopgirls looking insolently the other way
whenever one asked them for something. But it
was cheap. I loaded up with three days' shopping
and carried it to the car, which was only three hundred yards away. It was dark by now, although the
car headlights along the dual carriageway kept me
a cheerless company. I reached the front door and
looked around as I fumbled for the key. But there
wasn't anything, not even a shadow.

And yet, next day, I glanced around anxiously on
my way to the car. After work that evening I left
punctually, while it was still quite light, and was
glad to reach the security of my home, again while
it was still quite light. My mother was surprised to
see me back so early. "You aren't having any diffi-
culties with the office?" she asked.

"I prefer to spend a little more time in the evenings with you," I replied, and she gave me the
remnants of a once-splendid smile. It cheered me
all the same that I was loved dearly and needed by
one human body. I was beginning to feel lonely in
my predicament, perhaps because I couldn't talk to
her—not even her—about it. I settled down with
her to watch television. And yet I found I couldn't
concentrate; it seemed to me that if someone was
following me, he would know I was at home, with
my mother, and the room felt woefully vulnerable.
Above all, if anything happened to her . . . I went
off to check that all the downstairs windows were
locked and bolted for the night, and it occurred to
me how easy it would be for anyone to get in. The
thought had hardly occurred to me before, because
Farleigh had never been a town in which there was

much crime, although it had a very low-income area on its fringes. "What are you doing, dear?" my mother asked, when I got upstairs.

"I thought it was cold, so I was looking for an open window," I replied, dodging the issue. I took a whisky to bed that night, but even so slept uncomfortably. In the morning I wondered whether I was allowing myself to get run down.

Sunday was a cheerful day, with a bright sun, and I felt the need to get away from the town, away from the oppressive sense that I was under observation, to see if I could shake off the whole damn complex I was sinking into. I decided to drive out, into the country. It all looked very different, in the bright sunshine, from when I had been there on that terrible night. Old ladies chatted volubly, their bulky shopping bags on their arms in the village of Princetown, steeply banked up the hillside. A couple of long-haired louts in jeans lounged disconsolately about, as though they resented the sunshine. A young woman was pushing a pram, while her other hand was clutched by a cheerful-looking five-year-old girl to whom even I warmed a little. The street scene cheered me up, as I made for open country, and for the first time since the sighting on the bridge my heart lifted and my cares seemed to fall away from me.

The fields that ran to the top of the moor lay open before me. I thought I would drive a little, before settling down to a picnic lunch of a quarter of roast chicken, including the leg, which I especially relished, a delicious treacle tart cooked by my mother, and two cans of ale. Cooking cakes and pies remained one of her joys in life, and she could still do it, although she could not stand for long periods by the stove. I drove three or four miles on, into the barren part of the moor; it was very bleak and empty here: in place of grassy fields interrupted only by hedgerows and walls, and grazed upon by sheep, there was just dead red heather, mile upon mile of it, extending across very gently undulating country, with dips created by shallow streams, their tiny tributaries stretching out into the red, like the fingers of skeleton hands. There were no animals here, or farms, just birds wheeling high in the sky, mostly crows, some buzzards. It was empty and mildly depressing. Four miles across the moor, the country would suddenly plunge into a spectacular cliff formation overlooking one of the most beautiful valleys in the area, cradling the town of Arbuthnot. The road was a single-track one, meandering this way and that, in line with the contours of the moor. Not an easy drive at night, I reckoned.

To the left there loomed, in that bleakness, the huge abandoned hulk of Gilmour House. I had known it all my life, and yet it still made an impression. It had been the seat of some minor—and, judging by the location, eccentric—squire, built in the middle of the last century, a Victorian Gothic hulk, although not without a certain charm and lightness of touch; the stone, in particular, was of that weathered grey-blue that adorned the finest country houses of that underrated architectural epoch. But to come upon a large house in this total emptiness was a little unsettling. It looked forbidding, like a skull or an empty shell, in its hunched majesty upon the skyline.

As children at school we would be taken there; we were fascinated by it. It had been purchased by a hotel chain intending to make it into a conference centre; but the plans had come to nothing and it had been left empty. Yet the owners had generously allowed the school to use it as a base for groups being taken out on treks across the moors, and I well remember the empty interior, with its uncarpeted floors and seemingly endless corridors. The house was boarded up now, although I believe it was still owned by the same hotel group, which could not get it off its hands. You could see its giant shape on the skyline for miles around.

The road zigzagged across the moors, and then dropped sharply when it reached the cliff edge. There was a little clearing there, where you could get out and enjoy the scenery. It was a truly splendid day, with a bright, dark blue sky and a wind ushering the few clouds as though seeking to clear it. On the spot where I stood, I overlooked a row of serrated, ribbed cliffs, curiously circular and parched in appearance, like the edges of a jam tart. They plunged down three or four hundred feet into greenery below. Your eye could follow the line of a small valley leading into the larger valley of the Dear beyond, where Arbuthnot was cradled, half hidden by a hill on which an ancient fifth-century fort was perched.

The main valley looked green and distant and enticing, clusters of trees obscuring the river far below. On the far side, the thick, steeply wooded slopes of the Breare range made a pleasing contrast with the brightness of the sky. I took in the view, and drank in the air, and felt free, free of the city,

free of the worry, free of the meanness of man far
below, as I knew I would. The absence of my fellow human beings was what made the place so
wonderful.

Reluctantly, I went back to the car, ate my picnic, and began the descent into the woods below.
The road ran steeply down the side of the drop and
soon reached the edge of the trees. I encountered
only one car, but that was more than enough.
There was nowhere for him to back down to, so I
had to back up the hill to the nearest passing place;
the old Anglia was not that trustworthy on hills,
especially in reverse. I followed the road on down
to where a stream poured across it; a sign told me
to test my brakes after I had driven through. The
Anglia was low-slung and the stream fairly full, so
I did; the brakes seemed unaffected.

The road curved down the base of the cliffs, following the stream into the hidden valley, and I
soon came across a familiar landmark: an old Tudor
home in which Queen Elizabeth the First was supposed to have been hidden away when Bloody
Mary was on the throne. I was sure the story was
bogus, but I must say it looked the part, with its
fine weathered brown timbers, its tall windows,
and its still imposing chimneys hidden in that lush
green valley. The house was still a private one,
used as a farm, so I couldn't visit it. But I pulled in
to the side of the road and admired it. I looked up
the little narrow valley, the surroundings un-
changed for centuries, where green oaks merged
with conifer forest up the hill, and savoured true
inner peace: I resolved, yet again, to live in the
country, one day.

Then a movement caught my eye further up the hill and I froze. I literally found myself rooted to the spot for an instant. Where the road I had come along climbed up to the forest, there was a fairly level stretch in its ascent up the mountainside: someone had been standing there, silhouetted against the green, until I had raised my head. Then he had disappeared. It was just like the man on the bridge—he had moved because he didn't want to be seen. If he had just stayed there, I wouldn't have noticed him, or taken him to be admiring the scenery, like myself. But he had moved, to avoid my gaze.

With hardly a moment's hesitation—I did really want to find out who he was—I jumped into the car, turned it round, and started the climb back up from the valley floor. But I wasn't the sort of driver who puts up much of a chase, and the Anglia wasn't the sort of car to catch up with another, particularly on an uphill stretch. It wheezed its way up the country road to the ford. A car was parked there—a Renault—but there was no one about. I thought I glimpsed a movement in the trees beyond. I stopped my car, and without thinking plunged on into the undergrowth. Yes, I could see something—something moving in the trees.

Suddenly fear overcame me. Did I want to press on, to find out who my pursuer was? I had never been in a fight in my life. Suppose he attacked me? Who was he? Curiosity overcame my fear and cautiously I pressed on. Judging from the rustling in the grass ahead, the movement was of a strong, rhythmic quality, as though some kind of heavy job was being undertaken, like sawing up a tree. I found a shelter behind a tree and peered through the foliage. I almost cried out in astonishment; on a tartan blanket, a fully dressed man was moving up and down on a girl whose skirt lay pushed up around her waist. The movement was quite regular, and quite violent, but my attention was caught by the expression of glazed ecstasy on the girl's face, as she lay in a heap of rumpled blonde hair. He had his back to me, and his body reminded me of nothing so much as a mechanical pump.

I shrank back from being seen, a feeling of alarm mingling with my sense of guilt: the man had probably been looking out to make sure no one else would come across them; my phobias and worries had been beginning to unbalance me. Every suspicious movement was now interpreted by me as potentially hostile, potentially that of a pursuer. Before, I wouldn't have ever realised I was being watched.

Also, seeing a couple in the natural act of love like that depressed me. It reminded me of what I had never had, never could have: young love; to be attractive to a girl like that. Love! Was that love, that ugly mechanical act? I knew I had engaged in it. Sex was just the fulfillment of a desire, a brutish animal desire in the lower reaches of one's body; all that lad wanted was to fulfil his pleasure, at that girl's expense—although she had looked as though she was enjoying it, judging by her face. But that wasn't love, that was selfishness. Love was what I felt for Mummy and what she felt for me, because it was unmotivated, unselfish: we cared for each other as people, not as objects of desire.

Returning to the car I felt suddenly angry that

people should put their indecency on public display, in a place where they could be seen by anyone. The countryside belonged to everyone, it was not theirs in which to perform private acts that embarrassed the chance rambler.

Still, I was free of the sensation of being watched, and was determined to enjoy the rest of the day. Further down the enchanted valley, the road joined up with the main road, which swept down into the centre of Arbuthnot. The town was prettily placed across the river Dear. It had been spoilt a little by the tourist trade, which had converted every house in the centre into a little shop selling knickknacks, crafts, sweets, little mementoes of the place. Today, it fairly swarmed with life, families of holidaymakers spilling off the pavements onto the streets, cheerful and carefree in the sunshine. I was affected by their high spirits.

I parked the car in the nearly full municipal car park, then decided to round off my day by going to visit one of the sights of the place, a little black-and-white house where two old ladies in the eighteenth century had held court, entertaining the leading literary and political figures of the day. There was a whiff of immorality about the relationship, but they were well connected and dozens of important people of the town had come to sample their hospitality and to discuss the finer things in life. The house had always enchanted me, and appealed to my fascination for history; it was very old, and its ceilings so low and its doorways so narrow that it seemed built for miniature people. I examined the many letters on display from the ladies' voluminous correspondence; the place gave a wonderful feeling of period, and there were not too many people visiting: the crowds preferred to amble up and down the main streets looking at the junk in shop windows.

I emerged into the cool of the evening after that splendid day, strolled across to the car and drove off. It was only a matter of minutes before I realised there was something wrong: the steering pulled me sharply to the right; I had a puncture. There was no such thing as the perfect day, I decided wearily. I got out and had a look. The tyre was flat; luckily I had not yet reached the main road, so I was able to change the wheel on the spot. But it was a long, laborious process. I am hardly a very physical type, and not very good with my hands. I had difficulty finding the right spot to insert the jack in the mud-caked bottom of the car. Turning the jack was easy enough, but then I couldn't get the screws off the wheel. Some wretched mechanic had tightened them up too hard. It took me fully twenty minutes before I could exert the sort of leverage to get the last of them off, and I was bathed in sweat by then.

Fitting the spare wheel on was easy enough, though, and I was soon on my way. I decided that I deserved a drink after all that effort, which had left me feeling full of aches and pains but quite healthy, and I pulled in for a pint on the way back. I didn't get home until nine-thirty, after dark, feeling gloriously refreshed and rather depressed at the thought of going back into urban life.

My mother was pleased to see me, and made me feel guilty about being away for the day, as usual. But she made me tell her exactly what I had done,

as always; I omitted only the bit about the couple
in the wood. We had our tea rather late; she had
already had hers. I joined her by the television set.
The news came on.

The Hammer had struck again. Always he came
back to haunt me, when I had expelled him from
my mind. . . . The victim was the second non-
prostitute, a seventeen-year-old trainee nurse making her way from her lecture theatre to her hall of
residence before dark. It was the first time he had
struck in daylight. She had been clubbed down in a
field often used by students as a shortcut from the
main teaching complex to the residential ac-
comodation. She had been, in the words of the
commentator, "sexually assaulted and savagely mu-
tilated in the manner usually associated with the
Hammer."

The attack had been an unusually vicious one,
indicating that he had had little time to carry out
his grisly deeds, almost certainly because it was a
field often used by students, and one where he
could be spotted easily. The body had been discovered by another girl, walking alone; she was now in
a state of shock at the local hospital. The time of
death was established as approximately nine-seven-
teen, just a few minutes before the second girl had
reached the scene. It was possible to get the time
nearly dead-on, because the body was still warm;
the murder must have been committed literally
minutes before.

Inspector Prescott came on afterwards, looking
drained and white and angry. "This latest killing
underlines the fact that there is a monster at work
in the midst of our community. There is a very sick

and dangerous man at large out there. Please, if you are sheltering him, consider that it would be for his own good, and that of the community, if he is apprehended as soon as possible." When asked if he had any new leads, the inspector's reply was a tight-lipped "no comment."

"The news is always so depressing these days," said Mummy.

"I couldn't agree more," I replied, getting up and taking my plate out into the kitchen. "It's as if the public gloats over the whole Hammer business. I don't know what they'll show on television once he's caught."

"You wrote a paper about it, dear," she reminded me.

"Yes, but that was of historic interest, a scholastic work," I said in a mildly piqued tone.

Next morning I slept a little late: I suppose it was the fresh air that made me sleep so wonderfully well. I was dead as a dodo when the alarm went off, and had to rise and dress hurriedly, because the message didn't register at first. Never, in eighteen years with Palmer and Palmer, had I been late for work, and I wasn't going to be now—but nor was there going to be a hair out of place in my usual attire. When I had finished dressing and washing, I planted a kiss on Mummy's cheek, told her there was no time for breakfast—she usually prepared it because she always woke up much earlier than I did, and breakfast was easy for her to prepare.

I more or less ran downstairs, took my coat off the stand, and wrenched the front door open. It was only when I was three quarters of the way down the garden path that I noticed the two men at the end waiting for me. I pulled myself up, somewhat breathless. They were rather lean, grim-faced men in nondescript raincoats, middle-aged and hard, like most police detectives.

One of them said, with an effort at a smile and being jaunty, "You've cut it a bit fine this morning, sir. We thought you'd be out twenty minutes ago."

I drew myself up as though I didn't even know they were police, "I'm afraid I don't understand."

"Frank Haynes. CID, sir," he said apologetically. "I'm sorry, but I wondered if you'd come with us. We've got the car parked around the corner, where it won't be seen. Inspector Prescott told us we weren't to bother you inside your own home sir, and suggested we wait outside for you. I don't think you'll find this takes very long."

"But I'm already late!" I exploded.

"Can't be helped sir. But you can ring your office from the station," he said helpfully. "As I said, shouldn't be long."

I had no alternative. And I experienced no inner reaction, to my own surprise. I wasn't frightened, or indeed anything. I just prepared myself for what was ahead. There was no point in doing anything else. I let them accompany me to their car, praying that mother wouldn't be looking out of the window (of course she wouldn't—she hardly rose from her chair these days without a good reason, unless she had been anxious that day that I might be late). Anyway, I couldn't do anything about it. I hoped that none of the neighbours—not that I spoke to them often—were looking.

The car swept down the street. I was almost dis-

appointed that the siren wasn't on. I didn't ex-
change a word with the men accompanying me until one of them leaned forward to the other as we
approached the police station and said, "Only another eighteen this morning."

"You must be very busy," I said.

"Every time he strikes," said the second man
with raised eyebrows, "it's the same." That somehow turned me cold, as though I hadn't believed
my being picked up was in any way related to the
Hammer. And yet of course I knew. What else
could this have to do with? I was still a trifle
stunned, not taking in the enormity of what was
happening. I, who had hoped to leave the whole
saga behind, was being brought in for questioning
because a murder had been committed. I could not
quite believe it.

When I arrived at the police station, it seemed
anticlimatically ordinary. They brought me in,
past the desk where a sergeant didn't even look up,
down a long whitewashed institutional corridor,
and into a small study, cluttered with filing cabinets and papers and chairs summoned around a table. "The inspector'll be here in a moment, sir,"
said the jovial policeman. "Won't keep you very
long. Would you like a cigarette?" I declined, gazing distastefully at the girlie calendar above the
desk. "You can ring your office, if you like," he said.
"As I told you."

"No thanks," I responded. I wasn't going to explain to old Palmer that I was in a police station. I
could tell him that the car had broken down or
some such; but I didn't want to lie too brazenly in
front of these men.

The door opened and Inspector Prescott came in. He looked even smaller, greyer, older, wearier, than when I had first met him. He seemed distant, as though he didn't know who I was. He sat down at the desk, ruffled through some papers, and came across my name. Then recognition seemed to dawn, and a slight smile lit his face. "Harry Denman? Glad to see you again, sir. Would you like a cigarette?" he asked unnecessarily. I declined again, a trifle coldly. I didn't say anything. He lit one up for himself and leaned forward on the table.

"Well, I hope we won't have to detain you too long." In his office he was another man, self-assured, unhesitating, as pleasant as he chose to make himself. His authority made me recoil. "We've had to bring in a great many people for routine questioning." He puffed at his cigarette, not nervously, but as though drawing strength from it; his eyes narrowed as he did so. He seemed imbued with nervous energy, entirely different from the man who had interrogated me meticulously, almost diffidently, after Eileen's death. It rather shook me.

"You've heard about the latest murder?" He didn't wait for my reply. "Would you mind telling me where you were between six and nine o'clock yesterday evening? Please describe your movements as accurately as you can remember; and please list any witnesses who can corroborate your version at each stage." I began to describe my journey in full detail; it had left a pleasant and enduring afterglow. But I became aware during the telling of it that there had been almost no witnesses to confirm I was telling the truth. On any other day of the week, there would have been colleagues at the office, Mummy . . .

The others were watching me expressionlessly, their faces heavy, square, suspicious, capable of reading the worst possible motive into everything, as they had done all their lives. I told them about the incident of the couple on the hill, to add authenticity.

Prescott's face hardened, and his eyes narrowed with concentration. "But why did you go back up the hillside? That's what I don't understand; when you had just come down."

I could see what he was driving at. I reddened. I hadn't wanted to tell him I suspected that I was being followed. It would only complicate things further. "I thought I saw someone up there. I went up to take a look."

"You saw a rambler on the hillside and followed him up? Do you take an interest in such people? Hasn't he the same right as you to enjoy the countryside?"

"They weren't enjoying it. They were disporting themselves—spoiling the enjoyment for others by behaving like that."

"Yes, but you couldn't have seen that from the valley. I understand you're no stranger to the delights of the fair sex yourself," he added dryly.

I blew up. "Really!" I said heatedly, glaring at the other two. "That was in private. This is no place to make remarks like that."

"This is a murder enquiry, sir, and anything can be brought up. In strict confidence of course. Still," he said, looking at me, his eyes softening a little, "I apologise if it caused you offence."

"Don't I have a right to my solicitor being present?"

"You do," he admitted. "But these are preliminary enquiries only. We're trying to eliminate you from the investigation. You're in no sense under arrest, or even under formal questioning. We're not taking notes, even. I'm just trying to clear my own mind. Nothing you say will be used against you."

"Then tell these gentlemen to leave," I said sharply.

He pursed his lips and pointed towards the door surreptitiously with his hand and with a shift of his eyes. They went, slowly. "I'm not trying to be difficult," I said, to mollify him.

"I know," he said. "These things aren't easy. Tell me again why you went up the hill." His eyes, which had been fixed on the desk, suddenly switched to gaze directly into mine. I found myself surrendering.

"I had the impression I was being followed."

He didn't show a flicker of reaction. "Go on."

I told him about the man on the bridge. "It's strange," I added, trying to draw comfort from the sympathetic expression on his face. "Since that night when that poor girl was killed, I've been more uneasy than usual. I can't explain it. I suppose I must have taken too much of a morbid interest in the Ripper case for my history paper."

He nodded. "Who do you think is following you?"

"I don't know," I said honestly. "I thought it might have been one of your men. It wouldn't have surprised me if you were still suspicious. But my pursuer seemed rather clumsy. I didn't know what to think. If he was one of your men, you've got enough evidence that I was there on Saturday."

He puffed at his cigarette. "It wasn't," he said shortly. He asked me to continue with my account. At the end of it he said, "Apart from the couple in the bushes who you—er—observed, there's no one to corroborate your story anywhere along the line?"

"The ticket seller at the entrance to the ladies' house might remember me," I said hopefully.

"Will she?" he asked archly.

"Probably not," I said truthfully. "But then I wasn't seeking to construct an alibi for myself."

"No, that's a fair point," he said wearily. "And it might reassure you to know that around a third of the people I interview don't have alibis. All the same, I'd like to eliminate you from the enquiry early in the day, to save you time and worry, and ourselves. On the evidence, I can't. It seems almost unimaginably unlucky that your tyre should have burst just at that time, delaying your return."

"You don't have to tell me that," I said with a touch of irony. "I can't say I welcomed it at the time."

"No doubt it was tiresome. I believe you, and I'd like to spare you further difficulty. But we may have to ask you to come back at some stage for a further chat." He smiled briefly and economically. "I hope not," he added, and held out a hand.

"I'm wishing I'd never heard of this business, much less written a historical tract about it," I said bitterly.

"I'm sure Eileen would echo the first sentiment," he said dourly. I left him, unsatisfied with my performance. I hadn't dispelled the suspicion about the latest murder, because I couldn't; I quite genuinely had no alibi. This time, I had to trust the ability of the police to guess at the truth. I had much less contempt for them now that I was afraid of them.

In the office the two secretaries glanced up when I came in, then glanced down at their work again. Young Palmer gave me a brief look as he went past to greet a client who had just come in after me. Old Palmer asked me to cross into his office to look at the Old Rawling's Road deal. "This is beginning to be a habit," he growled.

But I knew how to handle him. "I'm afraid my mother hasn't been well. I had to wait for the doctor to come." Old Palmer's wife was poorly, and made him a soft touch for the health problems of others.

"I'm sorry to hear that," he said, and we talked about the contract. All the same I'll swear he was looking thoughtfully at me after I'd turned to leave the room.

Mummy was as well as she always was these days— that is rather frail, but nothing actually wrong. She pointed to a small parcel when I came in. "A present from an ardent admirer."

I went into the kitchen to help myself to the stew my mother had prepared, picking up the package on the way. I wondered who it was from; it wasn't office business, anyway: the address was rather carefully printed out; we had all the office business typed. I couldn't think who else could have sent it.

I opened it cautiously, as I put a pot of water on to boil the beans. There seemed to be no letter inside the papier-mâché envelope, just some article inside. I laid it down because I had to put the stew into the oven to warm it up. I was very particular about warming the oven before putting anything into it. It made a difference to pastry, in particular, making it crisper and more brittle.

Impulsively, I opened the envelope so that the article inside would slide out. When it didn't I rapped it on the table. The thing didn't come out, so I put in my fingers. A shock rushed through me at the soft, glutinous feel of it. I threw the thing from me, in that first reaction: it had the unmistakable texture of human flesh.

I drew myself up and picked the package up, where it had fallen on the floor, opening it gingerly and shining the light into the packet. It was an ear, a human ear. I could feel nausea beginning to rise within me. I had to catch myself, or Mummy would come running into the room. But I knew I was going to be sick. Clutching the envelope, I rushed off to the loo; my innards were rising in my mouth, and I only just made it in time. I kneeled, panting in the bathroom, the door locked, the awful thing in my hand, the sour taste of vomit in my mouth.

I heard a feeble knock. "Dear, are you all right?"

"Of course I am. Just something I must have eaten. I'll be all right in a minute."

"I don't think you had better eat the pie, then," she said with quavering maternal authority. Her footsteps receded. I gazed with loathing at the awful packet on the floor. There was only one thing I

could do with it. I had no intention of driving halfway across town to dispose of it in suspicious circumstances. I picked it up, dropped it in the lavatory, and pulled the chain. It was flushed away.
The full horror of just how deep, and how much
deeper, I was getting into this appalling mess, began to close in on me. I sank dispiritedly, wearily,
onto the edge of the bath, by the towel draped over
it, trying to think.

I couldn't think, because the thought at the very
back of my mind, the fear I wouldn't admit even to
myself out of sheer physical cowardice, as much as
anything else, had been confirmed. My watcher
was the Hammer. His had been the red Cortina; he
it was who had watched me from the bridge. He it
was who had followed me up onto the moor and
watched me from the hillside. He it was who had
shrunk out of sight when I had looked up at him.
He it was who had slashed the tyre to delay my
return. And then he had committed his murder,
knowing I had no alibi, in haste, with the utmost
brutality, because I might be back at any moment
and my alibi reestablished. And now he had sent
me a sign, a mark. Was it an attempt to incriminate
me, to plant evidence, or just to frighten me? I
couldn't be certain, but I thought the latter. My
whole frame was sick with the horror of what was
happening.

I didn't sleep well that night, and was decidedly
off-colour and on edge next day. So much so that
old Palmer, who was notorious for not taking an
interest in the welfare of his employees, looked at
me paternally from under his bifocals. "Are you

sure you're all right, Harry? Haven't been piling too much on lately?"

"Of course I am," I said shortly, and then regretted my touchiness. He had been trying to be kind, and I had given him no further incentive for being so. I absorbed myself in my work, because I didn't want to work through the implications of being pursued by the Hammer. I didn't know what to do about it, I didn't want to know about it, or how it had come about. I didn't want to face the terrible reality, I wanted to shut it clean out of my mind.

Only as the evening drew on did I start having to think. I didn't want to leave the security of people, of the office. I didn't want to be alone anymore. I didn't want to be the only one left in the office, where he could come and get me. I didn't want to have to walk alone to where my car was parked. He was probably watching every move I made, watching and waiting. I had to keep with people. After the office I could go to a pub. But when that closed, I would be at his mercy, back at home, with only my mother to protect me, and that was worse than no protection at all.

A chilling thought struck me. Supposing he decided to get at me through her? She was all alone, for most of the day. I had abandoned her: he could strike any time. I had brought this monster to her very front door—he had known, after all, where to send the ear—and I had left her defenceless. The hot surge of blood to my forehead began to cool. How could I protect her? I had to think. I must think, coolly, rationally.

Calm down; he wasn't out to get me. He couldn't have been—or he would have had plenty of opportunity to strike. No, he was playing a game. He was trying to frighten me, to lead the police to me. Why send the ear otherwise, except to plant a clue on me? And the whole sudden logic of what had happened on Sunday dawned on me. He had been following me for days, to see when he could pin a murder on me by choosing a time when I had no alibi. No, I wasn't in any physical danger, and nor probably was Mummy; he was trying to pin his murders on me, and wanted me alive. The thought didn't reassure me.

"Harry—have you finished the deeds on the Sloane property yet?" The question had been put to me gently by young Palmer, who had been watching me with interest for some time. I realised I had been staring into space for minutes.

"No, just a minute," I mumbled, snapping out of my reverie.

He glanced at his watch. It was five past five, and he would be wanting to get along to his evening's entertainment—to his girlfriend, no doubt. I worked slowly and carefully through the papers, keeping him there for ten more minutes. I glanced at him as he entered it in the books; the others had all gone. At least he was company. I got my own things together, closed up the safe, and checked the locks. He glanced at me; I could see he was anxious to get the business done before I was ready, otherwise he would have to talk to me all the way down the road, to my car. I decided to prolong the agony, by offering him a drink; it would take my mind off things. "Off to the fleshpots?" I asked jovially, as he rose to go, and I made to accompany him.

"That's right," he said, with the shyness of a younger man.

"I don't know where you get the energy." I locked the door carefully behind us. "Can I offer you a drink?"

"That's very kind of you," he said unhappily.

"Business certainly seems to be going well," I said cheerfully. "House prices are up eighteen percent on a year ago—that's seven points higher than the rate of inflation. Isn't it extraordinary how these little booms come along . . ." I burbled on, and he listened politely, mentally calculating how many drinks he need stay with me for.

We had nearly reached the end of the street. There were three men there, in a huddle on the corner. Abruptly I recognised one: one of the goons that had picked me up for questioning yesterday morning. I turned, suddenly conscious that we were being followed. Two more men were walking along at a discreet distance. I wanted to rid myself of young Palmer. I knew they were there to arrest me; the police car was parked just around the corner. I said to the boy, "I'm sorry, I'd forgotten I was meeting these gentlemen."

The one I had recognised stepped forward. "You remember me, don't you sir? I wonder if you'd mind coming with us. Otherwise . . ."

I interrupted him. "Of course. Anything I can do to help." I turned and smiled at the bewildered youth, who was gawking on the pavement. "I seem to have become an instant expert for the police," I said. The officers didn't say anything. They looked grim as I got into the car, two of them piling in beside me, one in front. The expression of puzzled dismay on young Palmer's face was the last thing I saw as the car sped off with a sweep and jerk that threw me back in my seat; its lights were flashing and its siren was wailing.

"Am I under arrest?" I asked mildly.

He didn't look at me. It was as though he was afraid he would do something he couldn't control if he did. He said, "No sir. It's a routine inquiry."

"With this many men?" He didn't say anything. At the police station, I stumbled up the steps ahead of the others, down the now familiar corridor to the now familiar office. They made me wait half an hour before Inspector Prescott turned up.

He was matter-of-fact, and didn't look me in the face either. He said, "I'm sorry to see you here again."

"So am I," I said quietly. "Is there anything new?"

He nodded, pulling a paper out of his drawer. He showed it to me: it resembled a graph, with fuzzy little bars where there ought to be a continuous line. It didn't mean anything to me. He showed me another: it looked to all intents and purposes identical. I raised my eyebrows.

"Voice prints," he said. "Wouldn't you say the two strongly resemble each other?"

I had to admit they did.

"One of them is a print of your voice. We taped it, I'm afraid, surreptitiously, when you were here in this room. The other is that of the Hammer, from the tape that has become famous around the country." I didn't say anything. There was nothing I could say.

He went on "There are slight differences, if you

look closely, but only slight. Now of course your voices don't sound the same: but the voice print identifies the underlying character and timbre of the voice. There isn't anything conclusive about them," he added wearily, "so they're not of themselves incriminating evidence in court, in the way that fingerprints are, for example. It is possible that two entirely different people's voices can have similar patterns. But it would be unusual. And I must say in this instance it strengthens what until now was a very circumstantial case against you."

"Am I under arrest?" I asked quietly.

"No," he said firmly. "You're free to go. We'd need a lot more on you than we've got before we would consider arresting you. This is one case in which I'm not going to risk arresting the wrong man. But it'll help us—and you, if you're innocent —if you'll answer some questions. And we'll need to search your house."

"I'll answer the questions. But I'm afraid a search is out of the question, for my mother's sake."

He ruffled through the papers on his desk, and put one in front of me. "I'm afraid it's necessary. That's the warrant. You don't have any choice in the matter."

My heart sank. It was over. Mummy would come to know. I didn't say anything. He began to question me at length, taking me over old ground, meticulously entering new ground, taking notes. I answered mechanically. I knew what my movements had been that Sunday, he couldn't shake my story. It was when he went back over the events of March 7, the night of Eileen's death, that I had to prepare myself for traps. I don't think I said anything inconsistent with what I said then.

His eyes watched me, after he had told me I could go. Outside in the corridor, the thickset man, whose name I had learnt was Sergeant Roberts, said, "We'll accompany you home, sir, as we have to make a search."

I said wearily, "Can't I get there before you, so I can take my mother away and spare her the unpleasantness?"

He shook his head. "No sir, you could take evidence away then, couldn't you?"

"Well, why don't you accompany me there, then let me take her out," I said in exasperation. "She's a frail old lady." He said he would ask the inspector and disappeared down the corridor. He returned ten minutes later. "That'll be all right, sir."

I steeled myself on the journey home; this time, thank God, the police weren't flashing their lights. It would be unpleasant enough as it was. My heart seemed to shrink into my boots as we walked up the garden path, and I let him in. We ascended the stairs, me calling as cheerily as I could. I opened the door to the living room on the first floor, and the sergeant followed me in. "I've brought a visitor, Mummy."

It was so unusual she looked up, startled. "Oh, but I'm not prepared," she said crossly, reaching for her spectacles on the table and pulling herself up.

"It doesn't matter," I said. "He's a policeman. He's not here as a guest. He wants to look around the house; I'll explain it all to you. Meanwhile, it'd be better if you came with me down to the Casa

Porelli, where I'll treat you to a meal, while he gets on with it." She hadn't been out for a while, not since I had driven her to church on Sunday; and she hadn't felt strong enough for a meal out then.

She fussed and flapped, as I knew she would. "But they have no right to search our house!" she protested, and the usually feeble eyes suddenly blazed. The veins on her thin hands stood out, as she tried to stand up. I helped her up, but I knew that there was no stopping her.

"I'm afraid we do, madam," said the sergeant, showing her the warrant.

"This is my house! You can't just come in here and poke about without my permission!"

"I'm sorry," he said, quietly standing his ground. How many such scenes had he witnessed in his time? He was professional, unmoved.

She turned to me, more bewildered than angry now. "But what is this all about, Harry?"

"I'll tell you when we get to the restaurant." I had decided to take her to the most expensive restaurant I knew, where we usually celebrated birthdays and anniversaries. She hadn't been there for months now. It was an Italian place, very cheerfully done up with Chianti bottles hanging from the ceiling and fish nets on the walls. She liked Italian food, and she liked the cheerfulness of the waiters, who made a fuss of her, helped her on with her coat and escorted her slowly down the stairs, although she always liked to make a show of independence and tried to descend alone. When I didn't give her a steadying hand, I was ready in case she fell. We walked out of the door, and she looked a little bewildered by the light. She hadn't been out in ten days. I walked her down the garden path to the car.

There were two uniformed constables eyeing us, a discreet distance away. Did they have to come in uniform, for all the neighbours to see? My eyes watched with black fury and despair. I knew she would feel it, like a spear through her pride. I helped her into the passenger seat of the Anglia, and we drove the ten minutes to the restaurant. The Italians recognised us, as always, and beamed and fussed. That seemed to cheer her up a little, although she still didn't say anything. We sat down and she scrutinised the menu through her glasses, and gave her order in a faint, firm voice, like the first cry of a small bird.

After the waiter had gone, she looked at me. I took her hand. I said, "I'm sorry, Mummy." And suddenly the anger and pride in her eyes seemed to go, melt into fear and concern for me. She seemed to take in that it was me that was in trouble, that that was what the search was all about. Her indignation at the violation of her home fled before the understanding that something was going terribly wrong with me. I swallowed hard. "It's not anything to worry about. The police are making exhaustive enquiries into the latest Hammer killing. Part of their enquiry is a check on the unmarried men in town. As I am known to have an interest in the case, I'm on their lists. They're searching the place as part of a routine enquiry. It's not anything to take seriously. I think they're absolutely daft, the way they're going about it. A bit more detective work, instead of these routine, plodding investigations, would get them their man. But it's just routine," I repeated inconvincingly. I sweated with the effort of lying. She didn't say anything, just looked at me with those wounded, concerned eyes, and I could see that she didn't believe me.

"It's more than that, isn't it?" she said at last.

I took a deep breath. "They questioned me, along with many others. They discovered I had no alibi on the evening the last girl was murdered, on Sunday—that is, when I took a drive into the country."

She frowned sweetly. "That seems very silly. I don't suppose anyone knew what I was doing that day. Why shouldn't they suspect me?"

"Yes, Mummy, but you're not the type who goes around murdering young ladies of ill repute."

"Well, nor are you," she replied. That was unanswerable. I smiled. We ate the rest of the meal in near silence. I could see that a terrible concern had settled on her, and she repulsed my few attempts to get conversation going on other subjects, to distract her. At the end of the meal, she gave me her slight, wan smile and heaved a little sigh. She walked to the car unaided. I drove home, hoping they would be finished. But they weren't. They had parked a van outside, and I could see the uniformed constables going up and down the path, carrying things. People were in their gardens, watching with interest. I said, "It's not finished yet. So I'll take you on a little tour." I drove on past, and could see her looking bleakly out of the window. I took her on my old route out into the country, and as the day was an in-between one—there was no sun, but little wind, and it was quite warm—I suggested she might like to stretch her legs.

"I don't think I'm quite up to it, dear," she said.

So I opened her car door, to give her a chance to get some air, and walked about a hundred yards and came back. I climbed in and we drove back. When we reached home, there was no sign of the police or of the van. I led that thin, bony person who was all I had in life up the garden path again, and though there was no one about, I had the sensation that every window in the street was looking at us. When we reached the drawing room, the place looked tidy, but all the familiar bits and pieces were a little out of place, in a way one noticed: it was as though our privacy had been defiled.

The drinks were in place, and I helped myself to one. Presently she said, "I think I'll lie down. It's been rather trying." I was pleased; I wanted to be left alone, to ponder difficult thoughts, and not to worry, as I did when she was in the room. I'd tried to sort things out in my mind, and couldn't, so I took drink after drink until I fell asleep in my chair —the first time I could ever remember having done so.

The dawn illuminating the windows of the sitting room awoke me. I rubbed my eyes, surprised when I realised where I was. I felt slightly soiled at the thought that I had gone to sleep in my clothes. I had to change them before going to work. Then I remembered all the terrible things that had happened to me, and wondered whether to go to work at all. Of course I should: to keep up as normal a life as possible was the best policy under the circumstances. I went to my bedroom, took off my clothes, and had a bath before putting on new ones.

I felt refreshed by that. It was only as I was about to make breakfast that it occurred to me that my mother hadn't got up; she was always up before me, usually at the crack of dawn.

I knocked on the door of her bedroom. There was no sound. I knocked a little louder and, hearing nothing, turned the handle. The familiar little room came into view: the curtains were drawn, but I knew every detail in the half-light: the comfortable, wide, double bed she had refused to change since Daddy died; the small dressing table, overladen with bits and pieces; the oversized wardrobe and chest of drawers, into which she tidied every article of clothing she had ever had. It was a room that almost seemed to represent her, to represent a life. But now that life was gone.

She was untidy in death, and that made it worst of all; she had fallen out of the bed with a look of pain on her face, as though she had tried to reach me, to cry out. Her nightdress was still caught up in the bedclothes, which had half accompanied her to the ground. I ran forward, but the expression on her face left no doubt. She would not recover. I wanted to make her comfortable, as though it mattered in death. I pulled her back onto the bed and closed her eyes, and tried to shut her jaw, but that wouldn't move. And then I broke down, half on her, half beside her, and wept.

I don't know how long I lay there, feeling her grow cold, except where I warmed her. I had always known this would come sometime, but I had always assumed it would be years hence. My mind could not cope with the fear that I had brought this about, so I consoled myself with thinking that I could not, would not, leave her. Only after what seemed hours did I get up and look again at the stiff little figure, so immensely frail and bony and wan and pathetic and small and inert on the bed where I had left her, just a tiny little form and a head on a pillow too tensed for rest, and sadness overwhelmed me. I went to the front room and mechanically rang up her doctor, whom I asked to come straight along.

"Is it an emergency?"

"I'm afraid I think it's too late."

"Then can you wait just an hour? I've got three calls which really are urgent. I'm very sorry. Very sorry," he added. I went back into the bedroom and sat in a chair looking at her.

At length the doctor came with a grave demeanour. He examined her briefly and said, "It seems to be a stroke. I'll write you out a death certificate; do you know of any undertakers?" I only knew old Jacob. I said I would ring him. "Good."

He took me gently but briskly through the formalities, then asked me how I felt. "Fine," I said, irritated at the question. She was dead, and he asked how I felt.

"Good," he said, looking at me intently. "But sometimes these things do affect one, a little after the event. If you feel at all strange, please don't hesitate to give me a ring." He got up. "It's the easiest, most painless way to go," he said, "although I know that's not much consolation." He left me then.

The funeral took place two days later. They had taken her away only an hour after I called, to a chapel of rest, where I had gone to visit her: she was stiff and waxen. She was as different as a statue, and I didn't linger. I insisted on a church service, because until she became incapacitated she had always gone to church. There was no room in the little cemetery of the church she used to frequent, so I had to take a plot in a much bigger, more impersonal graveyard, dominated by a rather forbidding church building. It wouldn't mean much to her in death anyway.

In church, I didn't feel so much unhappy as empty: the coffin looked so small in that huge cavern of a place with the rather poorly coloured Victorian stained glass which diluted the sunlight into a watery beam. There were only five of us there: one set of neighbours, with whom we hadn't got on too badly, and the former owners of the corner shop she used to patronise when she was still well enough. Her brother Jack had sent a letter saying he was too unwell to attend. I was infuriated; it seemed unbelievable to me that he could abandon his only sister to a lonely funeral. The music was depressing: a dreary dirge played with toneless finality on the church organ.

The vicar had a sonorous, pompous voice with which he delivered a sermon based on the few things I had told him about her and then added, somewhat patronisingly I thought, that those who lived a simple life were those God cherished most. I supposed by that he meant she hadn't done all that much, after Daddy's death. But simple was hardly a word that described her. I found I was cursing myself for not feeling more miserable. They often said that grief hit you later. But I couldn't find this hollow service, with its transparently bogus mixture of prissiness and sadness, moving. I just wanted to get it over with.

Outside, I felt differently, though. I had almost hoped it would be raining and cold, so that I could bid her farewell knowing that she was probably passing on to a better state, or at least tranquillity. Instead the sun was shining in a clear blue sky and a row of beech trees near the wall of the cemetery were green and splendid, casting their shadow on the well-cut grass; the singing of birds in the trees and the buzzing of flies reminded me of life, and how she had clung to it and what she was leaving. The undertakers had provided bearers for her coffin—at a grotesque price, I thought, for the whole funeral package, especially considering Jacob was a friend—and as they set off for the graveside, the finality of it all came home to me. The hole in the ground, the mound of earth made me realise she would never stir again. I had lost my only responsibility, my only companion. And I had been the cause of it all. From that search of the house, the certainty that I was in deep trouble had been too much for her. The whole chain of events that had led to her death had started in that seedy little prostitute's house hardly a mile away. I had let her down, and now I had no one and nothing to live for.

As the chunks of earth fell carelessly on the box, I turned away and said goodbye to the few that had come. I did that by the graveside because I didn't want them to notice the two men watching me from a distance, grim-faced. One was Inspector Prescott. But I think everyone saw them anyway. I glanced at the rapidly filling grave, at the speed with which the gravedigger was working. The vicar looked at me pityingly. "I'll stay a little longer alone," I told him. He turned to go back to his church, with a nod, as though he had been expecting a tip. The gravedigger winked at me. "Got the half day off; but I'll get it nicely finished," he said reassuringly as the earth was ladled in.

I went slowly over to where the two men stood. "Did you have to come, even to her funeral?" I said archly. "Why don't you arrest me, if you're so certain of my guilt?"

The inspector looked pained. "We're not following you, sir. I heard what had happened and came to pay my respects."

"It's your work," I said bitterly.

He was about to say something, but checked himself. "We won't be following you, sir. You have my word on that. I don't imagine you'll go far; where would you go? And anyway we're still at the enquiry stage."

"Did your search turn up anything?" I asked, half sarcastically.

"We're still evaluating the results of it, sir."

Yet, as I turned away from them to where my car was parked, I suddenly felt curiously disturbed by the policemen's assurances. If they weren't watching me, I was vulnerable to anyone else who might be. He might be, he would be. I couldn't voice my fears to the police, because that would be to give away the circumstances of Eileen's death. I was alone. I had cut myself off from protection by the law, and was prey to the lawless. At home, there was a package waiting for me with the same rather carefully formed writing on the envelope as before. I eyed it warily, as though it were a time bomb.

I made my way into the kitchen beyond the living room. There was no one there, and no one in the hall downstairs. It seemed utterly strange to enter the house and not hear a sound. She had hardly stirred from it in thirteen years; I was used to her every movement, her every complaint, the television interminably on, the weary cheerfulness as I came in. Instead, there was nothing. I thought the place would recall her presence unbearably. Instead the furniture, even the bedroom, was inanimate, rendered meaningless by her absence.

All was in order in the kitchen; there was no washing up to be done. The plates were in exactly the place they had been stacked, day in and day out, for twenty years; the cutlery, the glasses, the kitchen accessories, the washing-up liquids and brushes and the rest stacked away. The way she had ordered it. But now she was no longer there, it seemed almost meaningless. What was the point of order, when there was no one to take satisfaction from it? I filled the electric kettle and made a cup of coffee. I was a little hungry, but was also tired; the effort of going out to buy food was too much: there was bread and butter, and I found an old tin of Spam my mother had squirrelled away. I made myself a sandwich, and went back to the living room. More from force of habit than real interest, I switched on the television. There was nothing on the box. Just a dreary soap opera about a pub on one side, and on the other a tiresome chat show between four conceited individuals I didn't recognise, who were apparently media stars, full of themselves but otherwise empty. On the third channel a serious political programme about inner city housing in Bradford didn't interest me. And yet I left the set on, because its blare was company to me who had never lacked any. I had never been lonely; I knew other people considered me lonely, but as long as I had Mummy, I had a companion who filled my whole life; I didn't mix, because I didn't need any wider social life than her. Now I was lonely.

I picked up the package, and knew that a further stage in my persecution had been reached. Oddly, my sensibilities had been dulled by Mummy's death. The most important thing had gone from my life, even though that hadn't quite sunk in yet. Nothing else could be quite as bad. Why had I been so weak over the past few months? It was because I had been frightened she would get to hear. That it would affect her. Now she had heard, and was dead, there was nothing much worse anyone could do to me. What happened to me concerned me less than what had happened to her. I had no doubt this too would turn out badly, though.

What part of the anatomy had the monster sent me? The ear last time; what next? It had been an astonishing stroke of fortune that I had flushed the ear down the lavatory four days before, that I hadn't set it aside to dispose of later, for the police to find. This envelope, though, was an ordinary plain brown one, not one of those envelopes you use to protect delicate items. I opened it slowly; inside there was the familiar squat shape of a cassette tape. A chill ran through me. It was as though my every mistake, my every experience, was being

revisited, as though an attempt was being made to
ensure that every misdeed rebounded on me. A
tape; he knew about that, as he knew about everything else. There was nothing else inside the
packet. I picked it up gingerly and laid it on the
table. I went to the bathroom and found my little
recorder, taking out the Beethoven concerto in it,
and carried it to the sitting room. I put in the tape I
had been sent and placed it beside me.

It was crackling with interference, poorly re-
corded, with a metallic, dull edge to the voice. "I
think you're in trouble," it began. "I'm sure of it.
You would have got away with it if you hadn't sent
in the tape. I saw what happened because I was on
the streets looking for work. I saw what happened
and I felt sorry for you. Those damn whores. But
my pity couldn't continue when you tried to frame
me for what you did. Frame me; I've never tried to
frame anyone—anyone, for what I've done. How
could you do that? You read that paper. Even then I
didn't know who it was, until you appeared on television. And then I knew when I heard your voice
doing the Lancashire imitation. I've heard the tape
you sent a hundred times, but I keep ringing up the
police because it's so easy to, and I knew it was
your voice. I knew for certain that it was you that I
had seen scurrying, like a frightened rabbit, off that
building site. By the way, I went onto the building
site, you should know that, after you left. And I left
my marks on that girl. So they're certain the Hammer killed her.

"And yet you tried to pin it on me. You tried to
create an image for me. You wanted the credit for
what I had achieved, for my cleaning the streets.

Well, you may get it yet. But it's a question of who gets you first, them or me. I haven't made up my mind about that. But I will. Soon. I can lead them to you any time. What did you do with the ear I sent you? Or I can come to get you myself. What a silly fool you were, Harry." The voice clicked off.

The sweat was coming down my face, and my shirt was wet with it. I took the wretched thing out of the cassette. The flat seemed cold and empty and uninviting. For a while I just sat there, left to my thoughts, the sensation that I was in the grip of something uncontrollable. At length I stirred myself to make a cup of coffee.

That seemed to give me new life. I changed my suit and had a bath. I had to dispose of that tiresome tape, I thought dully, in case another search was carried out. It gave me something to do. I put on slacks, an open shirt, and a coat. When I went downstairs it was getting dark and I felt somehow furtive. My movements were being watched: clearly by him, maybe by the police, whatever they had said. How could I dispose of that tape?

I had an idea. The car coughed into action, and I turned it onto the dual carriageway, wondering which of the headlights behind me belonged to a pursuer. I wasn't going to outrun them. I wasn't made for that kind of cloak-and-dagger stuff. I drove two miles, taking a right fork into the centre of town.

The ungainly shape of the local cinema reared up. I went and bought a ticket, the tape still in my pocket. A film about martial arts in Asia was showing. A young audience was cheering and jeering at every movement, every leap, every thrust, every yell, every groan of these sleek, small dark men slashing away at each other with their hands. It would have been unbearably violent, except that there was no blood and as far as I could make out, no blows seemed to connect. It was anaesthetised.

It was indescribably boring, though, and I found it unbelievable that young people found such primitive things interesting. I remembered my own boyhood, reading books, studying, doing homework: but then I reflected glumly that mine hadn't been a particularly typical childhood. My contemporaries liked to engage in violence—I remembered with loathing some of the bullies I faced on the playground as a boy—but even they didn't come to see this sort of film. Their parents would never let them. Nor would the teachers. I felt a little conspicuous, as the only adult among them, as though I had gone in to watch a pornographic film, or with an eye to molesting one of the youngsters: it was more probable they would molest me.

I took out the pack of cigarettes I had bought at the counter on my way in. I took out one cigarette and lit it rather carefully with a match. I took care not to inhale, as on the few occasions I had done so, it made me cough. I puffed away at the thing. I could never understand what people saw in them: they had a pleasant enough aroma, and I had nothing against them, yet they had no effect of any kind on me. I had smoked half a dozen of the things before I estimated, in the dark, flickering half-light of the cinema, that I had enough room. Then I took the cassette out surreptitiously and pulled the tape out of it, winding it around my finger as I winnowed it out of its jacket for what seemed like an age, until I reached the end. It made a fine wrapping. I inserted the whole lot into the gap I had made in the cigarette box. I glanced around: there was still no other adult in the cinema. I couldn't have been watched. I endured the rest of the earsplitting, mind-numbing nonsense on the screen, then exited with the others. There was a large trash can filled with used popcorn packets and other detritus by the entrance. I popped the cigarette box into it, casually, as I went past. I had been observed by no one.

Outside it was dark and I felt at a loss. I didn't want to go back home to my flat. I climbed into the car. It was the only place where I felt really safe now. I clicked the ignition key on and began a half-hour trundle around the city, in search of a place where I would be utterly anonymous yet surrounded by people; people, to keep me from thinking about my fate as a man haunted, a man waiting on events, a man responsible for the death of his own mother.

I found a pub that looked a little better than the others in the working-class area of town. The lounge bar was deserted, however, when I went in. Self-consciously, I ordered a pint of beer. Feeling myself oppressed by loneliness in that bogus genteel place with its brass knickknacks, I decided to move into the public bar. The landlord, a large man with a cascade of double chins, eyed me curiously. Big men were in there, arguing loudly. I made myself as inconspicuous as possible with my drink, pressing into a seat by the door. In some way I drew strength and comfort from the company of these rough men. They argued, with force

and ignorance, about a variety of subjects, while I
stayed mute and watched. I drank one beer after
another, until I lost count and my thoughts trav-
elled from day-to-day matters, ascending into a mi-
asma of vague benevolence: the world wasn't such
a bad place after all; and this room was comfortable. And these were my friends, all of them my
friends. I wasn't lonely.

Friends, friends. A man sat down beside me.
"Anyone sitting here?" he asked rather reluctantly.
"Bloody weather, innit? For the time of year. It's
past September, and we're all bloody boiling."

I didn't want to get into conversation. I said, "It
is rather warm." I didn't want to have my vision of
abstract friends destroyed by the leaden personal-
ity of this man.

"You moved down here?" he asked archly.
"Don't remember seeing you here before."

"I'm just passing through."

"Hell of a place this town's become. Hell of a
place since that Hammer business began. We've got
it all on the brain. It's like a police state—coppers
stopping and questioning everyone. If I could get
my hands on that damn bugger . . ."

I wanted to change the subject. "You're from this
part of town, I gather?"

"Yeh. Where're you from?"

"Oh—Lancashire," I said, caught off guard.

He peered at me. "They say he's from there too."
He laughed. "You don't have much of an accent,
though, not like him. I'd like to be able to get my
hands round his neck. No women come into this
place now. Used to be full of them. Isn't that so,
Bert?" He looked up at a grizzled, unshaven old

man rather formally done up in a jacket and tie.
The old man reddened slightly. My friend slapped
his knee: "Christ, he'd done a few of them in his
time, and no mistake."

"He's a cheeky bugger," the old man told me. I
smiled and didn't reply. They both looked kind and
welcoming. I asked whether they might like another round. They said yes, and we drank three
more beers together, the two of them growing wit-
tier by turns, myself contributing nothing to the
conversation, but thankful for the company.

I felt rather unsteady as I got up to go. I had not
felt in the least drunk, sitting down, but I had to
make an effort to steady myself as I turned towards
the door, after time had been called at eleven
o'clock. "You all right, son?" asked the old man as
we parted outside.

"I'll be all right," I said. I moved towards the car,
trying to keep my balance. I couldn't care less now
whether anyone was watching me. I knew what I
would do if that damn Hammer dared to show his
face. I would kill him. I was strong enough, I was
sure of that. Somehow I got the key into the car
door and opened it. I slid in and switched on the
engine. The car began to move, and I found myself
beginning to feel sick. I jerked it into gear. I
wanted to get home fast. The movement of the car
was beginning to make my head spin. I pressed
down the accelerator and it roared into life.

A car coming slowly past flashed its lights at me
and hooted as I took my car onto the road. Bloody
fool. There was plenty of room. I roared ahead, my
foot on the accelerator. I had forgotten about the
turning to the left that led to the dual carriageway

until almost too late. I wrenched the wheel around, and a parked car suddenly came up to meet me, and then slid away. I was driving better than I had ever done in my life. Suddenly I was aware I was being overtaken, by a car with flashing blue lights. It slowed down sharply just ahead of me, and with difficulty I jammed on my brakes, to avoid hitting it.

I threw open the door of the Anglia. "What the hell do you mean, nearly causing an accident like that? You were following too damn close on my heels, weren't you?" Two uniformed officers were getting out, looking cold and apprehensive. They were so young and nervous I almost felt sorry for them. "Inspector Prescott, your boss, told me there'd be no one following me. Told me. You're disobeying orders. Unless he was just doing the dirty on me. It wouldn't be the first time."

They looked at me pityingly. Why? I knew what I was saying. There was something wrong with them, not with me. I knew what I was doing. One of them came forward with a bag. "I'd ask you to blow into this, sir," he said.

I roared with laughter. "Now come on. You're not going to get me on that one. You can't be seen to follow me, then try and arrest me on a drunk-driving charge. You're trying to set me up."

One of them said uncertainly, "I don't know what you're talking about, sir."

The other, more professional and a little older, said, "Are you refusing to breathe into the bag?"

I hadn't drunk that much. I'd call their bluff. "Of course not," I said. I blew. I didn't really notice what colour it changed to; it didn't seem to change

colour at all. I couldn't really remember what the
original colour was.

He said, "I'm afraid I'll have to ask you to accompany us to the station, sir. You'd better leave the
car here."

"Christ almighty! How am I going to get home,
then?"

"You could spend the night with us. Or a reasonable period of time, until you are fit to drive again,
sir."

I glowered at him. "I don't believe this. I don't
believe this is happening. You have no right to do
this."

"I must warn you formally that you are under
arrest, sir." He said it mechanically. "Please step
into the car."

I swallowed. "Very well." I went with him and
got into the backseat. "I'm beginning to know these
better than my own car."

They exchanged a glance. "Don't look so surprised. I know you've been following me."

"Sir, I don't know where you'd got that idea
from. We picked you up a mile and half down the
road, driving erratically. It's in the interests of road
safety," said the older one.

"Been in trouble with the law before?" asked the
younger man casually.

I didn't reply. At the station, they asked me
whether I would give a blood or a urine sample. I
considered a blood sample less undignified; but it
was a little painful. The sergeant was matter-of-
fact; he repeated the offer to stay the night "in one
of the cells. They're quite comfortable." I shook
my head. I wanted to get back to the familiar com-

forts of home. He said, "We'll test you out with another bag in an hour or so." They did, but it still went the wrong colour. I was starting to feel sick. They gave me a cup of tea and chatted among themselves. An hour later they gave me another bag, and this time I was free to go. One of them ran me up to where the car had been left. Now that I was less aggressive, he was almost cheerful. "These things happen," he said. "Had a row with the wife?"

"I haven't got a wife," I said irritably. Then realising he was trying to make things easier, I told him: "I buried my mother this afternoon."

"I'm sorry to hear that, sir," he said, tight-lipped. I felt a pang of sorrow towards a young man doing his kind of job.

The streets were empty when I got home, and again that awful sensation of loneliness pricked me as I opened the gate up to the garden path. I almost missed the company of the policemen. Once inside the front door, I bolted it, then noticed the envelope on the ground. I picked it up, and recognised the familiar awkward block lettering. Angrily I ripped it open. Why couldn't he leave me alone? A message had been composed from words cut out of a newspaper and pasted onto a piece of paper. It just said, "I think I'll save you for myself." I would have reacted, but I had no reactions left. I slipped it into my pocket, intending to burn it. I was upset; a metallic taste had come into my mouth, and I wanted something warming, something that would make me forget again, just as the beer had. I found our whisky and helped myself, and felt better for it. I drank another glass, and then another. I began to feel heavy and sleepy, and welcomed that.

I slept long past dawn that morning. I dressed hurriedly, feeling absolutely rotten. My head and all my limbs ached. It was all I could do to struggle downstairs to the car. Then I forgot my house keys, only remembering them by some miracle before I slammed the front door. There would be no one to open up when I came back. I set out at a quarter to eleven, an hour and three quarters late. When I got to the office, everyone glanced at me furtively. They didn't look at me after that.

I went to my desk with as much dignity as I could muster, and busied myself with a couple of properties. One of the secretaries came up. "Yes?" I said, over-sharply, and was conscious that everyone in the office, which was deadly quiet, was listening.

"Mr. Palmer would like a word with you, sir." He never usually summoned me in this way. Usually he came over himself. I walked the few paces to his office. He glanced up at me, indicated the chair with a nod, and slowly took off his spectacles, not looking me in the eye.

I had to break the silence. "I imagine you've heard what happened from William. Please allow me to explain. It was merely a routine enquiry."

"I don't want to hear," he said. "I'm only sorry to have heard about your mother. As for the rest, they're your personal problems and none of my business. What I wanted to talk to you about is our common business, this business, this firm we have worked so hard at together." I pursed my lips. In eighteen years we had never unwound in each other's company, always talking only of business. And

although he had been married, he had never invited
me to his house. That rankled.

"For a long time now, I've felt the business
needed young blood, a younger man running the
day-to-day work. It seems to me that William is
getting along very well, very well indeed. He's
competent, and alert, and popular with the staff.
He knows it all inside out. There comes a time
when the older generation must move on. The
boy's got plenty of new ideas. We're in his way."

"Arthur, he's a fine worker and an outstanding
young man, but he's still got to work himself into
many aspects of the business. If you're thinking of
retiring, I'm happy to provide the necessary con-
tinuity." I was thirty-eight. I had at least twenty-
seven years of working life in me yet.

"Yes, but let's face it, it isn't a question of age, it's
a question of a different way of working. You and I
were brought up in a period when being an estate
agent was a small, respectable, plodding business."

"We've built up a thriving business from nothing."

"People are much more competitive nowadays.
You need energy and youth and a much tougher
approach. We're just not up to it."

"What is it you're suggesting?" I was looking at
him closely now.

He seemed uncomfortable, which was rare in
that absolutely sedate, self-important, businesslike
old man. "I thought I would take a back seat, and
restrict my role in the business to a purely financial
one. I wondered whether you might do the same."

I was incredulous. My financial share was just
over a quarter, built up over the years I had worked

for the firm. The rest was owned by old Palmer—
51 percent of it, with the balance being held by his
son. If I gave up my managerial functions, I would
be left doing nothing—with, in effect, no say in the
business either. "But your role is purely financial
as it is. Except for the odd board meeting." Board
was hardly the word: it consisted of the three of us,
with old Palmer always getting his way; we only
had a chat about once every couple of months. My
role was to run the business. That was how we had
built it up.

"I think it's time to give William his chance," he
said stubbornly.

"In my opinion, he's not up to it."

"That's your view."

"That's my view."

He sighed. "Then I think we'll have to summon
a board meeting and decide. I might add that I
think we'll be prepared to make a very reasonable
offer for your share in the company."

I was flabbergasted. "What, you want to buy me
out as well?" He nodded. "What do you suppose
I'm going to do?"

"Oh, I'm sure you'll find something," he said
breezily.

"If you dismiss me," I said, controlling myself
with difficulty, "you'll have to pay a hell of a lot in
redundancy money." I was shocked by my own
language.

"I think the company can afford to give you a
generous golden handshake."

I was quivering with anger. "Well, if you're set
on it, I can't do anything. But my God, Arthur,
allow me to tell you you're an ass! I've built up this

company through my hard work and experience and knowledge of the market, and I can't bear to see some young idiot come in with a lot of trendy ideas and make a mess of it."

He looked at me absolutely woodenly. "My son is not an idiot. And my impression is that the company has been held back by your management of it. I think, if I may say so most respectfully, that you've been overworking, and that you've got rather a lot on your mind. I suggest you go on holiday when you leave the firm."

"Take a holiday?" I bridled. "Where would I go to?"

"That's part of the trouble. You've always pitched yourself too low," he said. "I suggest we call the board meeting for this afternoon, if that is agreeable to you. Then we can resolve the matter once and for all."

I returned to my desk. Everyone was looking at me, and no one spoke. I busied myself in trifles, and got through the day until the appointed hour of three. One of the secretaries popped out at lunchtime and got me a sandwich. I said hardly a word at the meeting, because I couldn't trust myself in front of that smirking youngster, with his mask of false anxiety, who had pushed me out. It was agreed to pay me a £15,000 golden handshake on top of the offer for my shares, which was generous, adding up to £68,000. I accepted the offer. "The value of the company can, after all, only go down now," was my last word. I spent the rest of the day clearing up my personal possessions. I had no obligation, and no intention of teaching young William the finer aspects of the business.

I was the last to leave, after all the others had said goodbye solicitously. I took a last look around the office, which had been as familiar to me as my home for the last seventeen years, which I had cared for as I would a child. I looked at the electric typewriters, under their covers, and the jumble on each desk, and the mugs for coffee and the comfortable yellow carpets I had had laid only the year before. I switched off the lights. I locked the door behind me and posted the keys through the letterbox. I was alone in the world now.

There was no envelope waiting for me at the house, thank God. I had got to the point of feeling apprehensive, as I walked up the garden path, in case he had some other treat in store. I bolted the door behind me and went upstairs. I helped myself to a whisky automatically. It was a movement that had become mechanical, although it hadn't been a few days before. I sank into a chair without switching the television on. I thought I would be depressed by anything I saw on it. I was deeply depressed anyway.

Suddenly all the anchors that had held my life in place were gone. What reason had I existed for these past seventeen years, except to look after my mother and to perform a useful service, to society as much as to my firm, by working? I strongly believed that everyone had his duty in life, that everyone had an obligation to work. Work contributed to the general well-being of society. Now I had no work; I had money, but nobody to spend it on. I wasn't going to lead a life of penury, but what was the point in having a house and money and all the time in the world and no one to enjoy it with?

Anyway, I was doomed. They were closing in on me from all sides. I glanced around the familiar room, and its contents seemed to provide no protection. He was probably watching outside now, watching and waiting, playing his little game. He was obviously enjoying himself teasing me, worrying me, playing on my fears. I wondered what it would be like to be killed by him. Just a tap on the head: I would feel nothing of what he did to me thereafter. But he wouldn't do these things to a man, surely? He wasn't that perverse. I didn't know. All I knew was that life would soon be extinguished, and I was glad. I was sick of life, which held out nothing but emptiness and guilt. I wanted to go, but I feared the manner of my going. I was frightened by the thought that the monster was waiting for me. I was too frightened to go to bed, to switch off the lights, to listen for any movement, any breathing. He was close, I sensed it. And I was sure now, after my experience with the breathalyser, that the police weren't watching me. They wouldn't protect me. You could always trust the bloody police to get it wrong: they'd persecute the wrong man, yes; but prevent a murder—never.

I went into the bedroom. I was afraid, very afraid, but I had to get over my fear. I had to get on with my life. I undressed reluctantly, and without clothes felt more vulnerable still, as though a murderer could slash through pyjamas and a dressing gown more easily than ordinary clothes. I pulled the bedclothes back. On the white sheet there lay a foot.

I reeled back in horror and shock, my stomach churning violently, my legs starting to sag. The thing had been neatly cut off, just above the ankle, and the blood on it was completely dry. It had small toes, like those of a little girl; she must have been a small woman. The red paint on the toes was chipped and faded. I noticed all the details as I looked at the ghastly thing. I noticed there was a note too. Slowly, with great care as if the foot might move, I picked it up. It contained words picked out of a newspaper glued to a piece of paper, as the previous message had. It said simply: "I paid you a visit and left my card. This one won't be so easy to dispose of." I fell to my knees. My legs just wouldn't support me anymore. I found to my consternation that my pyjama trousers were wet. I couldn't imagine how they had become so.

He had broken in, as easily as that, penetrated the only secure place I had. I was safe nowhere. He could pick me off at will. It was the violation of my living space, of my privacy, that was worst of all.

He might still be here. I lay there, listening hard. But I could hear only the sound of my own heart beating and the short breaths I drew for air. I climbed to my feet, and felt sickened by the thought of getting rid of the thing on the bed. I couldn't bring myself to touch it. Instead, I began to search inside the cupboards, under the beds, to check he wasn't there. He wasn't. Only then was I conscious that I was cold, and went and washed myself and put my clothes back on.

I wasn't going to sleep in the house, not while the possibility remained that he was still around. I had to escape the isolation, and the night outside was safer. I put on a coat and stumbled out to the faithful Anglia, my only friend in the world. It coughed into life, true to the last, and I steered it in the direction of the high street and main square, the old part of town, where my best friend—Wilfred—lived. I felt sure he would help me, and looked forward with affection to seeing that roomy, elegant old house with its period furniture and its aura of a bygone era. When I reached it the street was silent. I rang the doorbell; he answered after the second ring, looking a trifle irritable. He was wearing pyjamas and a bathrobe and slippers. He looked older and grumpier than I remembered him. It took him a moment to recognise me.

"I'm awfully sorry," I told him, unconsciously imitating his old-fashioned way of talking. "But I'm in a bit of a jam tonight, and I wondered if you could put me up."

"My dear boy," he said, not over-enthusiastically. "I'm very sorry to hear that." He realised he was keeping me waiting on the doorstep. "Come in, come in." I followed him in. "Can I get you a dry sherry? Very sorry. I never take the medium stuff myself. I don't have that many visitors." He searched a glass cabinet for the sherry decanter, took out two glasses which looked as though they hadn't been used in years, and offered one to me. "Now, what seems to be the matter?" he asked, for all the world just like a doctor. The cosy, stifling bachelor surroundings of his little study closed in around me.

"I've locked myself out of the house. Damn silly thing to do really. But ever since my mother died,

I'm not used to being careful about my keys, and I keep forgetting there'll be no one to let me in."

He raised his eyebrows. "Your mother dead? Very sorry to hear that, very sorry. I'd have come to the funeral if only I'd known. Splendid lady, splendid." He had never met her. "Can't you call the police?"

"I'm sure they wouldn't come. They've got more important things to bother about."

"Like locking you up?" he said suddenly. He chuckled. "I gather you're in some sort of trouble with them."

I flushed deeply. "Where did you hear that?"

"My friend Arthur Palmer told me. Had me to a drink the other day."

I was incensed. "It's completely untrue. Ever since I was picked up in a police car to give advice on the Hammer case, he's been spreading stories about me."

Wilfred grunted. "Yes, of course. I didn't believe you were the sort to get into trouble." He shifted uneasily in his seat. "But you can't spend the night here, you know. I haven't got a room prepared. Why, it's years since anyone stayed here. Mrs. Mathew"—that was his daily, who ruled him with a rod of iron—"would have a fit."

"Just a bed. That's all I need. I don't mind about sheets. It's just for the night."

"What about a hotel?" he asked, in some agitation.

"At this time of night? They'll all be shut." I looked at him, and sudden exasperation must have expressed itself on my face. What were friends for, after all?

He said rather weakly, "Oh, dear," and put his drink down beside him.

I leaned forward, alarmed. "Are you well?"

"It's nothing. Just one of these turns I sometimes get. I'm getting on in years, you know." He looked at me with wide eyes and a cautious look. And I suddenly knew what was bothering him, and it was so preposterous I almost burst out laughing. He added, "Besides, there isn't even a bed in any of the spare rooms. I had them all taken away."

I was annoyed by his attitude, and I forgot my manners. "I could always just sleep in the armchair here."

He didn't have an answer to that, but the thought troubled him worst of all. "Oh, dear. Isn't there someone else you could go to?"

He was in a terrible tizz, and the reason was that he was afraid of me. I could read it in his eyes. He had been convinced by what old Palmer had told him, and he feared he might have the Hammer in his house. To spend the night worrying about me— his heart might indeed give out. I said suddenly, with some contempt, "Oh well, if you can't put me up, that's all there is to it. I'm sorry to have bothered you at this time of the night."

Relief flooded into the old, hooded eyes. "Oh, I just wish I could. It seems ridiculous to have a big house like this and not to be able to put you up."

"It certainly does," I said dryly, draining my glass and thanking him coldly for the drink. He looked relieved as he followed me to the door, closing it almost with a bang as he muttered good night. I was alone in the cold again.

I had had an idea, while sitting with Wilfred, of

what to do next. He had proved a disappointment, not strong enough to stand up for someone that considered him a friend. So much for his old world courtliness. Inside beat the heart of a selfish man, determined to avoid any difficulty. Perhaps the reverse would be true of Eric, who for all his unpleasantness was hardly someone capable of being frightened by a physical nondescript like myself. At the technical college there would surely be a spare bed.

I didn't know where to go when I got there. The main building was a modern block with large plate-glass windows, surrounded by smaller buildings that could be laboratories or lecture rooms. I went to the main door, where a light was on, and pressed the bell. A sullen-looking porter glanced at me from the depths beyond a counter. He had been awoken. I asked where I might find Eric's house. "He won't want to be disturbed at this time of night."

"Please. It's urgent."

He peered at me suspiciously. "I dunno. There are so many of these lecturers. You'd better have a look through the list." I did, found the address, and thanked him. He gave me directions to the street, which was a quiet, residential one about a quarter of a mile from the polytechnic. I drove there. The lights of the big, rather featureless Edwardian semi were out. I had to ring the doorbell three times before I got an answer.

Eric was in a dressing gown, looking tired and jowly. He looked at me in astonishment. "Well, you're the last person I'd have expected at this time of night!"

"I'm terribly sorry," I told him in embarrassment. "It's just that you're the only one who can
give me a bed for the night. I can't get back into the
house."

The hallway was a disorganised mess of bicycles
and boots and raincoats. "Locked out? Well, you'd
better come in. Although why me?" He didn't
speak his unspoken thought—that we had always
been rivals, always disliked each other.

"I don't know. I can't seem to raise anyone else."

Through his befuddlement, he was amused. I
saw a woman in a nightdress beyond, peering
down the stairs. I was embarrassed again. "Sonia,
love, we've got a visitor," said the lecturer wearily.
"Make the bed in the spare room without waking
the children up, that's a good girl."

She didn't say anything, just went away to do as
she was told. "Come and have a coffee and tell me
about it."

He was so friendly, I was astonished. Suddenly I
began to trust him, to feel that for all his deficien-
cies, here was a man who was a real friend in need.
I said, "Do you really want the full story?"

"It's a long one, is it? Oh well," he yawned. He
led me into a kitchen done up in pinewood, as
though it belonged to an American log cabin. I followed him. I suddenly realised how tired I was, too
tired for sleep, anxious to share my burden with
someone. I didn't dare tell him about Eileen's
death. But I told him of the police suspicion, of
how my mother had died, of how I suspected I was
being followed.

His face was quite expressionless from start to

finish. Then he said: "So you *can* get into your house. Why don't you go there?"

"I told you, because I think I'm being followed, I'm being watched." And then suddenly I realised I *was* being watched—by his wife, or girlfriend, or whatever. She was standing in the doorway, looking at me thoughtfully. I flushed; I could hardly bring myself to tell Eric my story—but an unknown woman!

"I hope you don't suspect me too," I said suddenly, thinking aloud, remembering Wilfred.

"Of course not," interrupted Eric. He laughed self-consciously. "I can't imagine anyone less likely, if you want to know." He exchanged glances with his wife. "Are the kids still asleep?"

She nodded. She had a curiously intent expression, which made me uncomfortable. She came forward and sat down beside me, not by her husband. I was surprised. She said, in a quiet, controlled, sympathetic voice, "You're being followed by the police, and by the Hammer. And you think Wilfred thinks so too?"

I nodded, alarmed at how closely she seemed to have been following my story. I wasn't really accustomed to women who spoke for themselves. I had only just met her. She said, just as quietly, "Did you have this feeling you were being followed before your mother died?"

I thought for a moment. "Yes," I told her.

"And she had been ill for a long time?"

"Not ill, no. She had been getting a little frail, that's all."

She exchanged a look of satisfaction with her husband, as though she had been proved right. She

leaned forward: "Harry—it is Harry, isn't it? Eric's
always talking about you. Harry, my job is as a
psychiatrist attached to the teaching staff at the
polytechnic. That's where we met," she smiled
good-naturedly at Eric. "Harry, I want you to try
and believe me. You're not being followed by anyone. I know it's difficult to accept, but you're not.
When one has lost a relative, particularly a very
close one, it's not in the least uncommon for the
chemical balance in one's body to be disturbed,
leading to the most worrying changes in one's
thoughts. Yours is the kind of problem I come up
against most frequently. It's something that passes,
and usually passes rather quickly. But it is very
worrying when it happens."

I looked at her, blankly. What was she talking
about?

"Now, I think it's very important that you
should return home and get a good night's sleep
there. Very important. You see, if you don't sleep at
home and discover for yourself that your fears are
unfounded, you'll find it even more difficult to do
so tomorrow night. And the night after. You have
to overcome your fears, and see that they're based
on nothing. And then you'll overcome them. So
you see why it's so very important that you stay at
home tonight." She looked at me so earnestly and
intently that I could only look back, perplexed. She
was quite mad. She turned to her husband. "What
do you think, Eric?"

"I think that's right."

"Please understand it's not that we don't want
you to stay. Nothing would give us greater pleasure. I've made the bed. It's just for your own well-

being." Sincerity blazed from her eyes. She was going to leave me in the lurch, for my own good. I could see that. She knew more about me than I did myself. It made me quite sick.

"Would you like Eric to accompany you to the house?" That was the secret, why he was so wet: he was under her orders.

"No thanks," I said. "I've got a car outside. You're right, of course. I'd better go. Thank you so very much for the coffee."

She beamed. "I knew you had the inner strength. Now, I want you to do something else," she said, speaking to me as though I was a child. "In the morning, I'm going to call one of my colleagues to see if she has time for a chat with you, to help ease your fears. It may be that you require medication of some kind, to help you over a difficult period. She can advise you on that. Will you promise me you'll go to see her?"

I nodded that I would, and fled the place. God save me from the well-meaning, who were in every respect worse than those who meant badly.

As I drove, I checked the mirror to see if I was being followed. There was no sign of a car on the empty roads. It was just past 2 A.M. There was nowhere to go but home. And yet my heart shrank with terror and despair at the prospect of the empty house with that gruesome thing in it. And then I remembered one last refuge, one last place where I might find shelter.

I hadn't been there in five months. But I found the street easily enough, and parked just past Number 33, no different on the outside to any of its neighbours, save for the thick cream curtains al-

ways drawn, even during the day. I had kept an eye
out for a police car, but saw none. It was probably
reckoned by them to be too late even for prostitutes, let alone for killers. I went up the little path
and rang her flat bell. After a while a window went
up and a voice called softly, "What do you want?" I
could make out someone peering down at me.

"Is Fleur there?" I asked.

"This is Fleur. Who are you? What do you
want?"

"Don't you remember me? I used to be a friend
of Eileen's." I could tell she was peering closer.

There was an intake of breath from above.
"Harry! Of course I remember you. Hang on a
minute." There was relief in the girl's voice.

When she opened the door and let me in, I could
barely recognise her. It was the same girl, with the
same kind of innocence and trust in her eyes that
used to make her so different from Eileen. But she
was much thinner than I remembered her, almost
to the point where she had lost some of her figure:
the curves of her breasts and bottom were slight,
under her nightdress. She seemed extremely
pleased to see me. When she had reached her floor,
she closed the door of the flat behind us. She said,
"I'm always worried sick when someone rings the
bell like that. You never know whether it might be
him. I've never recovered after what happened to
Eileen. Nor did the business. It's ruined my
nerves," she said. She was a torrent of words. "But
it's lovely to see you. Eileen was always so fond of
you. She thought you were a gentleman."

"I'm glad to hear it," I said. "And you're not
frightened of me?"

Her eyes widened for a second. "No. You were here on the night she was done in, remember, waiting for her. You couldn't have done it. That's one thing I can be certain of. It's nice to see a bloke I can trust. Sit down on the chair," she said, indicating a worn couch. "Drink?" she asked, with an attempt at professional coolness. I asked for a whisky. I smiled at her benevolently as she joined me, sitting on the arm of the chair. I kept a hand round her bottom. She ran her fingers through my hair.

"Who's in the next room?" I asked.

"No one. They haven't been able to rent it since Eileen died. It's got around that that was where she lived. They'll get someone, sometime, I'm sure. But people think it's got a curse on it or something. It's stupid, really. But it's very lonely here for me, that's the only thing. And I'm always frightened now. It plays on my nerves. It's very difficult with the clients, too. I can't just take on anybody, and it's not as if business was that good in the first place."

"How do you choose them?" I asked her gently.

"Just by the face. You have to trust them. You can tell. I don't go for the creepy ones anymore. That cuts out half the business." She looked wistful. "You're nice, anyway." She ruffled my hair and started to unfasten my tie.

I said, "Not yet." I felt no desire for her, and I hadn't come there for that anyway, just for shelter. She seemed surprised.

"I thought you enjoyed it directly. Eileen said you did."

"I'd rather just relax and talk first. I'm not in the

mood just now. Tell me, why didn't you move into some other line of business, when this one became so dangerous?"

She looked at me with a slight glance of disdain. "It's my profession. That's what I'm good at, isn't it? I don't want to do some boring job, like being a shopgirl. Anyway, there aren't any jobs." She had evidently considered a change.

"Why don't you get some—protection. A man to look after you?"

She giggled. "Not offering yourself, are you?" Then she turned serious. "Look, I'm short enough as it is. If I get a pimp in, he gets three quarters of the take. Even like this is better than having a pimp. Did I give you a price, by the way?" she asked, suddenly anxious, fearful I might leave when I heard it. "Twelve quid fifty, any way you want it, one go. Or thirty the night. For you I'll make it twenty-five." Just the same businesslike manner as Eileen. Only more nervous and more innocent. To her it was a business, just as selling houses had been to me. I had given of my time, and brains, for money. She was giving her body. That was the only difference.

Her body. I glanced at the pale thin shape under the nightdress, the spindly legs, the bright, pretty face that thinness had accentuated, not destroyed. I felt no stirring of desire for her, so different from voluptuous, blowsy Eileen. She was like a young girl, whom I would like to caress, to put to sleep, tuck in bed with a teddy bear, not make love to. Somehow Eileen had dispelled my sense of shame about the act of love. She had reeked of lovemaking, as though that were her main reason for existing, to be slept with. To do it with this girl would be to take advantage of her.

Misinterpreting my gaze, she peeled off her nightdress with a quick movement, shaking her hair back into place after she had discarded it. I was mildly stirred by her nakedness: her breasts were too small, and she was too bony; but the curve of her waistline, of her legs, held something. But then I remembered how my hell had started in this place, and how I had been atoning for my crime ever since. I hadn't come for this. She smiled, and leaned forward to unbutton my shirt. I said, "Not yet, I'm not in the mood."

She frowned. "Don't you like me?" She was puzzled, disappointed.

I said, "You're lovely, it's just me. I don't know what's the matter with me tonight. Listen," I added, "I'll pay you the rate for the night if I can stay here. Maybe I'll perk up a little later on."

"I can make you perk up," she said with a smile, leaning forward.

"No, no," I said hastily. "That won't work. It might come to me later."

"You can't stay. I've just remembered, I've got a customer." She looked anxiously at her watch, which was the only thing she was wearing. "He'll be here in ten minutes. I'll have to be quick if you want it."

My heart sank. I was going to be homeless once again. "What about the next room?" I asked. "I'll pay the rate for the night for that, too."

"What, just to sleep there?" she asked incredulously.

"To see if I get it back. Then, when your client's gone, I could come back to you."

She thought for a moment. "All right, but pay me in advance."

I didn't have enough money. I wrote her a cheque. She insisted that I write my card number and address and telephone number on the back. "Now, if you'll excuse me," she said pertly, as though I was a familiar and tiresome lodger. "I've got to get myself ready. Hope the room doesn't give you the creeps. I know I couldn't sleep there." She drifted off towards the bathroom.

I went to the room. It was terribly familiar and evocative. The bed just as Eileen had left it; the chair and the basin and the chest of drawers. Only the drink was missing. Just going into it, and losing the distraction of Fleur's presence, made me overcome with misery and fear again. I hated being alone. I was afraid of my thoughts. This was where it had all started. A few moments of squalor on a bed, a self-indulgence I had mistaken for pleasure, had led to the death of the one person I loved, the loss of the job that I valued, and had turned me into a hunted, persecuted fugitive, chased by police and criminal alike, with no home, even, to go to. I sank, clothed, into the bed and found my mind was spinning around. I couldn't even muster the effort to take off my clothes.

There was a sudden creak of the floorboards, and I turned. Nothing there. I found myself sweating. I pulled off my jacket, determined to force myself to sleep. That creak again; I turned. This time I swear I saw her standing there, in her voluptuousness, naked and laughing at me with that terrible look in her eyes the day we had fought. But of course it was all in my mind, there was no one there. Yet the image persisted, I couldn't drive it out. And then over in the corner I saw her again, and while the mocking grin remained, her eyes were empty and sightless, her hair matted with blood, as she had been when I had gone over to the body. Oh God, this room was so much a part of her, she dwelt in it even when she wasn't there—

This wouldn't do at all. It was all in my mind, of course. There was no one there. But I had to get out of this ghastly room. I pulled on my jacket again; I didn't want to run into Fleur. I opened the door gently and slid out, going down the stairs as quietly as I could. I was aware of movement behind me. I looked up, and she was standing at the head of the stairs, looking lost and bewildered through the powder and lipstick she had just put on. She said, "You're going already?"

"I'm afraid so. You're right—the room is—troubling."

I saw tears well out of her eyes and run silently down her face, which contorted in sobs. I ran up the stairs. I couldn't bear to see someone crying—I had never seen a grown woman do so. I took her in my arms and she pressed her wet cheek against my shoulders. I held her gently. "There, there," I said. "What is it?"

"It's only—it's only you've been so kind to me. And it wasn't because you wanted to sleep with me. You just wanted to be nice to me. Most men aren't like that. They're nice before, then they're like animals, then they turn surly and go. You were kind and gentle."

I didn't know what to say to that. I just kept on pressing her to me. Here was someone whose existence had been worse than mine. It was strangely comforting. But I wasn't kinder than anyone else, I knew that.

The doorbell rang. She looked startled. "That's him," she whispered. "Quick, get back in the room. He doesn't like to meet other men. He's very shy." She ran off to arrange her hair. I had no wish to meet him either. I slipped back into Eileen's bedroom and again the thoughts came rushing at me. I would get out the moment he had passed.

I heard her go down the stairs, to let him in. I heard the breathless welcome, the kiss, as she accompanied him back up, asking whether he had had an easy day. A soft, slightly whining voice replied that it was always hard at work. I had heard that voice before, and thanked heaven I had hidden from him: the last thing I wanted was to meet someone I knew in the place—a sentiment no doubt shared by Fleur's customer. After the door to her room had closed, I slipped onto and down the stairs and out into the cold rain to my car. I drove back home because there was nowhere else to go.

I had made up my mind, on the drive back, and it was with an unusually determined stride that I went up the garden path. If he was watching, if the police were watching, I didn't mind; they had lost their hold over me. The uncertainty, the fear of the unknown that had been with me, had gone for good. The logic of my position was crystal-clear. I was a man who had always prided himself on his decisiveness, on the ability to think a problem in the office through logically, make decisions without allowing emotion to cloud judgment. Now that I had come to a decision, I was astonished it had taken me so long to think it out logically. As I ought to have at the very beginning.

Admittedly, it was the most difficult decision of all: the most terrible. Yet if that indeed was the logical solution, so be it. Only logic remained now; my emotional commitment to life had gone when they had buried my mother. She was my reason for being, for living; now I had none. The judgment to be, or not to be, rested with me alone. As long as society had a use for me, the balance was that I should live. But society had no more use for me; and life, persecuted as I was by the police and by that monster and, worst of all, by my conscience, was intolerable. Why put up with it? There was no hope of respite.

The only thing that could save me was if the police caught the Hammer. But that might not happen for ages, if ever. I could not bear even another week of this mental agony. There was one way to cheat both the police and the Hammer—how angry he would be when he learned that I had escaped his clutches! How dismayed Prescott would be when the next Hammer murder took place—a murder I could not possibly have committed. The satisfaction I would derive from cheating those two men alone made me want to go ahead with my plan.

I thought first of hanging myself. That might be the easiest way. It would give someone a nasty turn, but it had the advantage of requiring only a simple act, kicking over a chair, to finish it. Then my problems would be over. But I had no rope in

the house, and besides I wondered if there was anything strong enough to tie it to. The only way
which was ready to hand was to take the sleeping
pills my mother left in a jar beside her bedroom
table. I was afraid of doing it that way. It could be a
long and painful process. I hated sickness and
stomach pains. But I concluded that I would probably only drift off to sleep. I went into her bedroom,
with its musty smell of mothballs, and found two
bottles of pills. I felt they were a gift from her.
Soon I would be joining her.

That was all nonsense, of course, I knew what
death was all about. It was peace, sleep, nothingness, merciful oblivion. There was no heaven, or
hell: in killing myself I wouldn't be condemning
myself to anything; I would just end the purgatory
I lived in in this world. I would hurt nobody by
taking my own life, merely cause a pang of conscience for those who deserved it. I owed it to myself to kill myself.

I poured the first bottle of pills into my hand,
then the second. There were about forty; that
would do the trick, surely. Suddenly I wondered
whether I should leave a suicide note, to explain
everything to the police, why they had been such
bloody stupid fools. They probably wouldn't believe it anyway; they would conclude I was the
Hammer—until the next murder came along to
prove them wrong. Let them make fools of themselves: I wasn't going to go through the trouble of
making things clear to them. I looked at my hand,
and quailed. I knew then that I would have to take
the pills suddenly, without thinking. Too much

thought, and I wouldn't take them at all. For God's sake nerve yourself, man.

And then the telephone rang. Its jangling tones rang through that room, pealing through the silence, playing on my nerves. I didn't want to answer. What was the point? I had resolved to make my break with the world. And then the thought crossed my mind that this was an unusual time to be rung up. I glanced at my watch: four-fifteen in the morning. Curiosity overcame me; I picked up the receiver. I expected to hear the banal tones of the police—or him. I could tell either that I was going to cheat them.

Instead the voice was that of a girl, a voice strangled in terror, gasping with tension. "Thank God," it whispered. "Thank God you answered." In the second it took me to recognise Fleur's tones, she said, "It's him. I know it. I can sense it. Please come quickly. Please. He's coming back from the bathroom—I've got to ring off. But please come."

The line went dead, and I sat for a moment, stupefied. Only for a moment. I leapt to my feet, and abstractedly poured the pills into an ornamental jar we had on the sitting room table. I put on my coat, flicked off the lights, and ran downstairs two at a time. I didn't think of taking a weapon, or what I would do when I got there. Something much stronger than myself had got into me now. I was in the car in an instant, and drove as I've never driven before, speeding up to eighty, straining the poor old Anglia. If the police stopped me now, I could but lead them to him. But there was no one else about. Not a single car, not a single person, no

lights on in the houses except the streetlights with
their sickly yellow glow.

I slowed down as I reached the Jericho district,
turning up the steep, narrow, terraced streets until
I reached 33 Querchmore Road. The building was
shrouded in darkness; I went to the door, and
found it open on the latch: a sickening feeling of
anticipation crept into my stomach. The house was
absolutely quiet. I climbed the stairs with dread,
and reached the door that led to the accursed flat.
He might still be there, watching me, for all I
knew. I was prickly with fear. I crept into the little
hall, taking care in the dark, not daring to turn on a
light. The door to her room was ajar; I pushed it
open, and could make out the shape on the bed.

I stood motionless for a moment. I didn't want to
switch on the light, didn't want to see what he had
done to her. It was enough to see the unnatural
way in which her body lay across the bed to realise
the hideous disfigurement he had done to her. Why
hadn't she screamed, the silly girl, instead of ringing me up? Maybe because the walls were thick,
and people probably wouldn't have thought much
of it, in this neighbourhood. Or maybe it was just
that she had been too frightened. People did
strange things when they were frightened.

Suddenly I switched on the lights and flicked
them off again as quickly. I got one glimpse of what
a madman can do. It was unbelievable; there was so
much blood: on the bed, on the walls, all over the
place. And her look of terror . . . I stood sweating
but strangely in control of myself. I had had to
witness that horror; not from morbid curiosity but

because it would nurture the feeling that was giving me new life, a new determination to live.

I closed the door quietly behind me and left the flat. Nothing stirred. Nobody had been awoken by the crack of his hammer on her skull or the appalling knifework he had inflicted on her.

Dawn was staining the sky as I turned the car up the hill, toward my refuge in the countryside above, and so remote from, the town, and the human concerns below. I stopped the car just off the little side road, climbed the gate, and went down the gentle field. I gazed out over the stream. I watched the whole sky growing lighter, and the sun coming up, a watery, washed-out globe in a clear sky that promised a fine day. In my veins there boiled a pure anger.

A girl's life had been taken. To me, life had been valueless; to her it was everything, in spite of its squalor. She had done no one any harm. She had made her living in the manner she knew best and now, in order to satisfy a maniac's blood lust, she had died. I had dispensed with my self-pity now. She had had none, and yet been treated pitilessly. I had a task in life, a destiny had unfolded itself before me: to see that this monster never struck again. I had been blaming myself for what had happened to Mummy, to my life. And yet far more to blame was that man who inflicted death and agony wherever he went. As I had nothing to lose, I must be prepared to risk my life in the process of ridding the world of him.

I gazed at the dew which moistened the carpet of green beneath my feet, at the gurgling, bustling, eddying stream below, at the trees in their panoply of green, rustled by a very gentle wind. It was quite cold at that time in the morning, even though it was late summer. All this was life. Who knew, I might even find a satisfactory way of living up here, regaining the will to exist. For the moment, my motive for living was fired by one thought alone: to rid the world of this man, to apply my mind where the police, in their mindlessness, had failed. God, what a selfish idiot I had been! Always bewailing my own lot, when other people were fighting for their very lives. It was the way the girl had spoken to me on the stairs that had particularly touched me. I had never heard a woman speak to me so gently—need me. It was as if she had had a premonition, as though she knew she would need my help. Why had she rung me up? Because my telephone number was ready to hand on the cheque. And I had failed her.

So I must think. I had enough clues, God knew, as to the identity of the killer, more than the police had, probably. I knew he was a member of our history circle on the night we had all repaired to the pub after my lecture. I knew he had a red Cortina. I knew his voice: I had heard it on the stairs. It was not a familiar voice, but I had certainly heard it before. I wished I could place it. I had to recall the meeting of the Society, to remember exactly who had been there. Most were friends: I jotted their names down on a piece of paper. I could not believe any of them was capable of such a crime. And then I remembered the two guests. But I could not recall that either of them had spoken.

Still, it was worth starting there. I had to find out their names. One had been a guest of Edward

Jones, who ran the supermarket chain; the other a friend of Jacob Stewart, the undertaker. I considered both of them my friends. I resolved to drive into town as soon as the shops opened and to make enquiries. It was much too early yet. I felt refreshed by the wind and the smell of the wet upon the grass. I began to draw strength from it. I felt sleepy, as I hadn't before. I decided to take a couple of hours sleep in the car. I lay in the back, and to my surprise was out like a light.

It was five after nine by the time I opened my eyes again. I was wasting time. I felt refreshed and climbed into the driver's seat. I was aware that I hadn't shaved. I must be a sight. I thought perhaps I'd better go home and make myself presentable. I drove straight to the house. As I approached it I noticed two police cars parked near it; there were big, burly men near the gate. I turned left down a turning a couple of hundred yards before I got there. Of course: I must have become suspect number one; they would have found my fingerprints at the murder flat, prints I hadn't troubled to cover up in the self-confidence my new mission had given me.

There was nothing for it but to go on to Stewart's place. It lay in a narrow street off the central square; it had a sober and understated front window, as was appropriate for the trade. I pushed open the door, and a smooth-faced young man in a dark suit sitting at a desk rose to greet me. He wondered if he could help me: I told him I was a personal friend of Jacob Stewart's. He went to find the undertaker. Jacob came in, looking quite unlike his cheery self at History Society evenings. He was long-faced and grey and unctuous. He turned a shade greyer when he saw me, and put on a forced smile. "Hello, Jacob," I said. "I shouldn't think you were expecting me."

"Harry! You're the very last person I expected to see here." He didn't ask me into his office, just stood there like a lemon.

"Can we have a private word?" I asked with a touch of irritation.

He recovered himself. "Of course. Why don't you come into my office?" He exchanged a glance with the young man at reception. "You'll stay to greet any clients, won't you, Robert?" He closed the door behind me. He said in a tense voice, "I really should call the police. In fact, I think I ought to. Please get out, Harry. You've come to the wrong place. There's nothing I can to do help."

"What are you talking about?" There was a quaver of anger in my voice. Had the whole world gone mad?

"Haven't you seen the papers? You've become the best-known face in Farleigh—in all of Britain. I'm just astonished that Robert didn't recognise you." He turned the *Daily Telegraph* on the table to face me. A photograph of me lay across two columns, with a small story saying that I was sought by police in connection with their enquiries into a series of murders in the small northwestern town of Farleigh.

I said: "I see. You don't believe all this, do you?"

He looked at me, and his eyes and face seemed to relax. "No, of course not." He looked shrunken in some way. "But please get out of here. You don't know how much trouble you could cause me."

"I've come for just one thing. That guest you brought to the History Society last time—what was his name?"

"Why do you want to know?" he asked sharply.

I decided not to tell him; he might go to the defence of his friend. "If you want me to leave quickly, tell me."

He searched his memory. "Of course. Ted Thurgood. Oh, he's a nice chap. I hardly know him, but he was interested in the case. He was a local government officer seconded from Blackpool. He's gone back now."

"Which department?"

"Social Services. Why do you want to know?" he asked again.

"He has some information that could be useful in my historical researches."

"You're pursuing your researches now, while the whole country's looking for you?" he asked incredulously.

"They're necessary to establishing my innocence," I told him mildly. "You're a very expensive undertaker," I went on. "My mother's funeral cost as much as a small car." I couldn't stand the frightened little man. "Goodbye, Jacob." I left him. I hoped he would be so frightened to admit to the police that he had seen me and not called them that he wouldn't summon them. I had one more port of call. I could do it on foot. It was just around the corner, and the policemen in the square would have a description of my car.

Edward Jones's shop was less than five minutes away, up a side street. It was a large, featureless, checkout-counter operation, with housewives pushing trollies mechanically past the checkouts where girls in blue smocks with little name tags saying MANDY and TINA sightlessly and mindlessly exercised their fingers on cash registers. I saw Edward in a white coat, making his way down the shop; in that thronged, yet anonymous, concourse I went up to him.

He too was surprised to see me, but controlled it well. "Harry. Of all people," he said.

"You don't believe what the papers say?" I asked.

"I don't know what to think," he said, with the honest, bluff manner that was his trademark. "Why are you here? Look, let's get out of the way of this lot and go into my office." Shopping trollies trundled past us.

"That won't be necessary. I just want to know one thing. What is the name of the guest you brought to the History Society when I gave my paper on the Hammer?"

He said quickly, "Baines. Ted Baines. He wasn't a friend really. He'd worked here for a couple of weeks with me after he lost his job as a fitter at Greenfield's plant. I took him only because he was unusually bright for someone in a job like that, and he always showed a keen interest in history."

"Where does he live now?"

"Why do you want to know?"

"I think he has some important clues to the identity of the Hammer."

He looked at me, and thought about it. At length he gave me the address. Then he said, "You wouldn't pull the wool over me, would you?"

"Of course not."

He smiled. "Then for Christ's sake get out of here. I can't believe you're capable of it."

I had my man. He was the only person who could have been the killer—other than one of my friends, and I knew them all too well for that. A feeling of triumph surged in me as I left the shop and made my way through the throng of early-morning housewife shoppers, and I found myself wondering if they recognised me from the pictures in the paper. Suddenly a pang of fear seized me: I had to get away from them! I controlled myself: they were hurrying to work. I realised none of them were looking me in the face.

All the same, I had to take care. I turned down where the car was parked. It had gone unnoticed. Did I dare to drive it? I considered the risks, and decided that to acquire any other form of transport would be still riskier. If I hired a car, or even took a taxi, I might be recognised. I only had one call to make.

My Anglia, my pride, started, faithfully as ever. I just prayed I wouldn't run into a police car in the ten-minute drive to the council estate where he lived. I knew the area well. It was a mile away from the red-light district, from Jericho. How he hadn't been caught baffled me: most of the murders had occurred within a two-mile radius of the place; surely the police, even in their plodding, routine investigations, had interviewed every householder there. The road drifted past me in a daze. I could hardly concentrate on driving. I was thinking of him, and of what I would do when I got there, and keeping half an eye out for a police car at the same time. They would all have been fitted out with descriptions of the car.

I switched on the car radio. I was item number three on the news. But no description of the car was issued. It was said that all routes out of town had been blocked; that was obviously where the police cars were concentrated.

I turned the car into the entrance of the housing estate. It was the same grey-brown sprawl of so many that had sprung up around the town. The house was semi-detached, with a pebbledash exterior and a wooded first floor like some bleak British transmutation of a Swiss cottage. Children were playing in the street as I drove up; most of the gardens round about were unkempt. To my surprise, though, Number 83 had a carefully cultivated front garden behind a low fence. There were tended flower beds, although the flowering was over that year; the lawn was mown; the rosebushes were carefully pruned. The house looked neat and tidy. A new door had been erected, made of some kind of varnished wood, which stood out a mile from the dreary doors round about.

There was no sign of a red Cortina in front. The day had turned into a fine, sunny one, which made even this drear neighbourhood seem cheerful. A few houses down, two mothers were chatting animatedly across a fence. Beyond that a few children were playing with a ball on the dead-end street. It was safe enough.

I walked with trepidation up the path. If the car wasn't there, the odds were that he wouldn't be either. I felt a little hot and uncomfortable in the warmth of the day. But I had to find out, I had to be sure. I had to find a clue, something decisive. If he was at home, I thought his reaction at my appearing on his doorstep would betray him. If he wasn't, well, perhaps I could break in and find a clue. Failing that, I would wait for the return of the Cortina and waylay him on the path. I had to be sure.

I knocked on the door. An instant later it was opened—by a woman. The thought that he might be married had never occurred to me. I suppose I could not believe that a woman-hating monster of this kind would be married. She looked up at me expectantly, surprised by my silence. "Yes?" she asked.

"I'm sorry to disturb you," I said apologetically, "I'm looking for Mr. Ted Baines."

"He's at work," she said without interest.

"Ah," I said. "I'm an estate agent." I had decided to lie professionally. "I'm calling because we've heard that there's a fine property in the road. A private house, and we've had some enquiries from people wishing to move into the area."

In the brief pause after I had spoken, I sized her up. She was small and nervous and wore thick spectacles. There was an intelligent look about her, and rather a remote and intense gaze behind the glasses, as though she had closed her mind to the things of this world, which she viewed with an intuitive hostility, and preferred to live in one of her own. She was in her forties, and was not at her best; her hair was drawn back severely from her forehead, nevertheless wisps of it strayed across her forehead. Her dress was a plain one, rather short above the knee, but so unstylish that I felt she

wore the length for practical reasons, not to make
herself alluring. Yet there was something undoubt-
edly attractive about her. It was her combination of
tension and warmth, which suggested self-posses-
sion, as though she was the kind of woman whom
the pressures of life could have made self-pitying
and yet somehow wasn't. As though she had tried
to fight back all her life.

She said, a little quickly, "I'm sorry. I don't understand."

"There are people who want to buy houses in
the area. Yours is a private one, purchased from the
council." You could tell that by the new front door.
"My clients are offering very good prices. I wondered if you'd be interested."

She hesitated. "My husband's away. But you'd
better come in." She had clearly decided I looked
respectable enough. She led me through into the
sitting room. It was comfortable and decorated in a
predictable way. There was cheap modern furniture: a settee, two easy chairs, a couple of wooden
chairs. The carpet was green-grey and rather deep.
The chairs were arranged around a table in front of
the television. There was a switch-on gas fire with
a logs-in-the-grate effect. It was all very tidy, save
for a newspaper lying askew on the table. There
were prints on the walls—one of Venice, the others
cheap prints of flower arrangements. There was
something at once defensive and human yet rather
synthetic and cheap about the place. I instantly felt
she was a lonely woman, glad of the company.

"Can I get you a cup of tea?" she asked, inviting
me to sit down.

"That would be lovely," I said.

"I'm sorry the place is such a mess. I've got my hands full with Jan," she said apologetically. She hurried off and returned with a cup. She didn't have one herself. Instead she led in Jan, a three-year-old girl, fair-haired, big-eyed, with that look of mischief and self-confidence that children of that age have. She looked at me coyly for a moment with wide eyes, then ran across the room and clutched my legs where I was sitting. I was always awkward with children. I patted her on the head and smiled nervously.

"Jan, you naughty girl—come here, love," her mother called. "The gentleman doesn't want to be bothered." The child looked to me for support.

"Oh, she's no bother," I said, and the mother looked pleased. "I was wondering whether I might catch your husband at home."

"It's very difficult to say. He has the strangest hours. He's a pest control officer with the council, you see. It just depends when he's on call. He has to go out at all hours. I thought he'd be in this morning because he had a late night last night. But they were on to the phone to him first thing. I really can't tell you when he'll be back. But you could leave your name and number and I'll get him to ring you when he gets back. But who would want to buy our house?"

"You'd be surprised. Some of these former council houses are in very good condition. You've improved this one since you bought it, haven't you? It's an ideal size, and it's well decorated. I'd say it would be very desirable."

"My husband did it all himself." She smiled and caressed her child's head. "Ted's very good with his

hands. I can't think why he didn't become a
builder. His carpentry's best of all."

"Really," I said. "I've been looking for some time
for someone who could repair my furniture. It
saves buying it new."

"Why don't you look in his workshop? He's got
plenty on show there. It shows the sort of thing he
does. Real craftsmanship. Don't mind the mess in
the kitchen."

It was a mess, a jumble of unwashed dishes and
an ironing board full of clothes she hadn't ironed
beside the washing machine. She seemed to be a
trifle scatterbrained. The garden had a small vege-
table allotment, and a large shed. Inside the shed
there was a set of cabinets, tables and chairs, like
the ones I'd seen in the lounge. The craftsmanship
was solid, if unimaginative. My attention was
caught by the tool rack. It was neatly and tidily
stacked. It contained saws, lathes, and other instru-
ments. A set of five beautifully polished hammers
was on the tool shelf, two of them with their ends
small and beautifully weighted, like industrial
hammers. There were spaces in the rack for two
more. I said, with an effort at sounding jovial, "It
must be a bit lonely, with him out all the time."

She looked at me, with sudden interest in her
eyes. "It is. But I'm used to it. I used to live alone
for a long time. That's always the way, isn't it, with
men: they're not stay-at-home creatures."

"Some men are," I said melancholically. "It
seems a strange combination, pest control and carpentry." She didn't say anything.

We were back in the lounge, and I sipped my

cup. "Have you been married long?" I asked con-
versationally.

"Four years. Long enough to get this little nui-
sance off the ground," she said, indicating the child
with a wave of her hand. She seemed eager to talk
about herself, like most lonely people. "We've lived
here ever since. I used to work myself, as a librar-
ian. That's where we met. He's such a gentle, lov-
ing man. I wish I could see more of him. But he has
to go out to work. He's very clever, but he doesn't
talk to me much." I was surprised she was telling
me so much. I warmed to her. She didn't seem to
mind in the least what she said; she was rather
vague, distant, friendly. "Anyhow, this can't be
very interesting for you."

"Will you tell him I called?" I said, draining my
cup. I gave her my card. The little girl came up and
grabbed my knee playfully. I said, "One other
thing. Has there been evidence of trouble in this
area—near the house? It makes a difference to the
price, you know."

She looked astonished. "Trouble—no. We've always got on well with the neighbours, although we
don't see a lot of them." She seemed slightly ruffled, and switched back to her vague, preoccupied
look. "Anyway, I'm glad you called, and I'll certainly tell him."

"Thank you for the tea."

I called with the same pretext two doors away.
The woman was plump, jovial, middle-aged, leaning on the fence outside her home. "I can't imagine
anyone wanting to buy one of these," she laughed.

"Is there ever any trouble in the area, though?

Vandalism, that kind of thing. Anything which might have brought in the police?"

"The police—no, we never see them. We're a forgotten corner. It's about time they paid a visit though. Some of these kids . . ."

"How do you get on with the neighbours? With Mrs. Baines, for instance."

"Oh, she's all right. She's not very talkative. They keep themselves to themselves. He's a funny one, though. He's always so quiet, never says anything; gives me the creeps. How she puts up with him with the hours he keeps! It's the only thing she ever complains about—she doesn't see enough of him. I suppose he's busy—but I can't think there are rats enough to keep him busy all that time."

I came away with a heavy heart. I had found my man, but his family knew nothing of his misdeeds. The truth would shatter his wife and child, just as it would have shattered my mother. I went back to my car at the bend in the road, parked it in a siding so that I couldn't be seen by the people I had just talked to, and waited, and waited. Not until five o'clock did the Cortina appear.

I watched him get out. He was insignificant physically, of middle height, with a thin frame and a shuffling walk. His face had a slightly intense expression, like that of a harassed schoolmaster, and a smile that seemed fixed in a grin it didn't have, as though he were trying to please someone he didn't like. His top lip was thin and a little prissy. He was as pale and nondescript as on the previous occasion I had seen him. He went into the house, looking dead ahead. He had no reason to suspect he was being watched. He wore a pair of dirty grey trousers, a check shirt, and a roadman's leather jacket, additionally padded for warmth.

So this was the cause of all my troubles. It seemed incredible. Seeing him in the flesh dispelled my fears. He was a human, and a very ordinary one at that. The Cortina had, however, confirmed that he was my man. I waited, with infinite patience, because I had only one thing to do now.

I switched on the ignition and drove slowly down that characterless cul-de-sac, taking the road that led up onto the moor. The sunshine had turned into a moody, sultry day, with low cloud that soon turned into mist, and the car swayed slightly under the impact of the wind. There was a light patter of rain that just satisfied the windscreen wipers. Their monotonous clicking punctuated the murmur of the engine as the car wiggled along the winding moor road, through the bleakness. To my surprise, I saw no police car. By the time I had reached the top of the moor, the land was enveloped in mist, scurrying in patches across the bunched-up heather mounds. I stopped the car and began walking down the short track that I knew led to the old house; I couldn't see it, but it was less than a hundred yards away. It was still light by the time I reached it, but the mist was obscuring most things. The ground-floor windows were devoid of glass, shuttered up with wooden boards. The big oak door I remembered had been replaced; wooden boards were up, chipped in a few places—where, it seemed, children had tried to break in. The place was desolate and I felt a little alone. I tried the boards, but they were securely nailed in, and I couldn't budge them.

I circled the house, and climbed over a wooden fence into a yard at the back. It was all boarded up. I could find no way in. Then I saw the ring in the ground in the large wooden trapdoor. I had to pull hard, and it came up. A flight of stairs led into the cellar. I went down, and poked my way about in the dark. It took several minutes to find a narrow wooden staircase leading upwards. I climbed it, and found my way barred by a door. I felt for the catch, and to my surprise it clicked easily upwards and the door swung open. I was inside; the dingy interior was dark, but it seemed like light after the pitch-blackness of the cellar.

I had to make a thorough search of the house before I found what I was seeking: an isolated room on the second floor; it had barred windows and two doors. The key to one was in the latch. I tried it on the other, and it fitted. The floor was bare; there was no furniture. I put the little tape recorder, with the blank tape inside, on the floor.

It was cold in the house, and I didn't linger. By the time I had found my way out through the cellar exit, darkness had fallen outside. I crunched my way down the stony path to the car. Then I drove down to where I had come, back to the cul-de-sac on the edge of town.

The red Cortina was still there. I parked my car in front of it; somehow I had to attract his attention; I wondered how to do so. The curtains were drawn, but around the edges there was light showing. He was in there, he wouldn't go out without his Cortina. I wondered whether to throw a stone at the window; but that would have been too obvious. In the end I got out of the car and gently opened the gate. I went across the grass, up to the window, as silently as possible. I peeped through the crack in the curtain. I could just make out a woman's feet beside a chair. I stood there, irresolute.

I suppose it must have been the sudden movement I caught out of the corner of my eye. I dodged sideways with a speed accelerated by the surge of shock and fear. I glimpsed the flashing metallic object slashing through the air beside me, and as I plunged desperately forward glimpsed a cruel face twisted in a grimace of pure hatred, teeth fixed, eyes murderously glazed. My heart beating like a steamhammer at the narrowness of my escape, I was over the gate in an instant with him only yards behind me, still clinging to his infernal instrument, an extraordinary agility to his movements. I dived into my car and switched the engine on; as I jammed my foot down on the accelerator, the window beside me shattered in an explosion of falling glass, and I glimpsed again the dark glint of the hammer, the snarling mouth, and the mad eyes.

Then I was away—I couldn't afford to let him overtake me until we got to my destination. I was out of breath, and my contempt for him had been replaced by a sensation of pure fear. In my mirror I saw his headlights being switched on in the distance. I had reached the bottom of the cul-de-sac, and turned up to the roundabout that led to the road that led up into the hills. I felt a sudden urge to take the second turning, which led back towards the police station. I was frightened. Then I reminded myself I had to go through with what I had begun if I was ever to be free.

There was rush-hour traffic about, and for a moment I thought I had lost my pursuer in the mixture of headlights behind me. It was only as I turned up the hill and began the slow climb that the confusion was resolved, and two sets of headlights came up after me. One turned off before the road flattened where it reached the moor.

He was no longer driving fast now, content merely to follow and wait for me to stop. I knew he could not stop me as long as I was actually in my car. It was eerie, going into the mist on that cold and empty moor with only a car behind me to keep me company. There was no comfort to be found in the brightness of those beams. My car wound its way across the peaty emptiness, its dipped headlights skittling across the surface of the road: the mist was so thick now I could see only a few yards ahead. The road was so winding that I had to swerve sharply sometimes when the road came up at me unexpectedly. His lights had become a general lightening of the mist; they were no longer visible. I didn't want to lose him, although I wanted a little breathing space, so I slowed down, and he came closer. I spied the rough track that led up to the house. There I waited for him until he slowed down before accelerating up the track. He thought he was the hunter, but I was leading him. I drove as fast as I could, as soon as I had seen that he had turned in after me; the road led to one place.

Once out of the car I didn't waste any time. I positioned myself at the side of the house; the air was cold and clammy with the mist, now that the wind had dropped a little. It left a curious feeling on the skin, as of being brushed by a wet flannel. I saw the eyes of his car grow brighter, and then he slowed it to a stop as he saw the bulk of the house and of the parked Anglia. I heard the door click open and bang shut. For a second I saw the figure of a man, and maybe only my imagination told me I could see his eyes, those eyes, the mad, demonic, piercing eyes shining above an inexpressive mouth —but that may have been my imagination, a memory of the man I had seen before.

The slight figure striding towards me, clutching two objects in its hand—that I did see, and it was enough. He had seen me; he mustn't catch me up. My heart pounding, I ran down the side of the house and around the back. I sensed that he was closing on me: he was a lighter man and faster runner than I was. It was rash and foolish of me to have exposed myself to him in that terrible, empty, cold, hard place. I found the gate, and was over it in an instant. I heard him struggling to get over it while holding onto his tools. I ran across the courtyard where weeds carpeted the cobblestones, past the junk that lay about in heaps, to where the iron ring lay. I pulled it with all my might. I left the trap open, and was down the stairs in an instant, thinking I could hear his pursuing footsteps. I plunged on into the deepest dark of the cellar, to the staircase that led up into the house. I paused. I could distinctly hear steps coming down into the cellar.

I climbed to the top and was soon in the house. It was pitch-black here too and I had to feel my way along the walls and up the flight of bare wooden stairs—this side must have been the servants' quarter—that led up to the second floor. I began my

climb, my ears straining to hear him: he was following me, wasn't he? Or had he got lost in the
cellar? I stopped and listened. Nothing; not a
sound; there was just myself in darkness in an old
abandoned house on the top of a moor with no one
for miles around but a homicidal maniac. It was
now that I couldn't hear him, now that I couldn't
pinpoint him for sure, that fear began to gnaw at
the pit of my stomach. I realised he could be anywhere—watching me, ahead of me, waiting to
strike.

I had to shake myself out of my mood; once I
started to fear, I would be finished. He couldn't be
ahead of me because only seconds before he had
been well behind me. He had probably got lost trying to find the way out of the cellar. I knew what I
had to do: I had to lead him, by making a noise as I
went up the stairs; to lure him up to the landing. It
was not far ahead, in the pitch-blackness.

Then I heard a noise ahead of me. It was unmistakably the sound of a man who had been trying
hard to suppress the noise of his quick breathing.
So he was there, on the landing, waiting for me. Or
was I imagining it? Was he behind me? If I turned
and ran, would I fall into his arms? Suddenly the
fear seized me again and my legs felt weak. I took a
step back.

Then a voice spoke: it was a quiet, measured, curiously toneless voice, that of a scientist or an ac-
countant. He said, "You made a terrible mistake,
Harry. You thought you would lead me onto your
ground. And instead this is a place I know very
well. I have used it as a refuge for many of my
operations. I like this house, and I know my way

about. Better than you do, I think. I came up the
main staircase and got ahead of you."

I had been edging downstairs as he spoke; a sigh
of relief swept over me now that I knew where he
was. I might have run into his arms otherwise. So
he knew the place; it couldn't be helped. I turned
and started running, and I heard his steps coming
after me in the dark. I ran wildly, at his speed, a
frenzied speed propelled by hatred and madness;
and then the noise behind me stopped. I stopped
too, and listened. I heard nothing but the sharp,
short breaths of the man. I strained to hear if he
was moving. I could see nothing.

I heard a creak, and I thought it the creak of a
step taken towards me. I couldn't be sure, I
couldn't tell anything in this darkness. I had to get
into his mind. Would he go on down, or go upstairs
across to the top of the house, and down the other
stairs, to get at me from the back? That depended
on what he thought I would do. If he realised I
would go back up the stairs, he would wait for me.
If he thought I would try to surprise him from
behind, he would come on down to get behind me.
It would depend on what he thought I would do;
but he would know that I would try to guess what
he would do. Damn! Damn! It kept going round in
circles. The reality was I was stranded in the dark
in an empty old house with a mad killer out for my
blood.

I heard a noise: it was very gentle and very close,
just the faint creak of a floorboard. I leaped down
the stairs, taking them three at a time. I heard a yell
and a jump after me; the monster had crept down
almost to where I had been standing, making no

sound. He was a master of stealth, with all the experience of stalking his victims behind him. I dashed across the landing, stumbling and somehow righting myself; I could hear him and the faint clank of his horrible tools against each other behind me. I reached the other flight of stairs and ran up them two at a time. Silence fell behind me; I knew I wasn't being followed any more. Still I pounded on up the stairs, desperate to get to my sanctuary, the barred room, the room of all my plans. The stairs seemed unending and I almost fell when I took a step into empty space on reaching the landing. I ran forward, oblivious of the noise, across to the door that led to my room.

I reached for the handle and found that another hand was on it.

What happened then was like a slow-motion film. I had time to reason things out in a flash: he couldn't have expected me to get there so soon, or he wouldn't be trying to slip into the room. He must have wanted to wait in the room for me to go past the door; he must have crept at speed up the back stairs to intercept me. His hand was not ready to wield his deadly instrument. I glimpsed the glittering eyes and the lips drawn back slightly in the beard, showing hard, cruel teeth, and then I lunged with my fist, and made contact with the softness of his stomach, which crumpled, and I felt a sharp sting in the side of the arm, as though it had been cut with a very fine instrument.

But his hand was off the door handle now, and mine wrenched it open and I plunged in, aware of the jabbing sensation in the arm, and the wetness and stickiness there. I staggered into the room, and drew the door behind me with a bang. I flew across to the other door as I heard him open the first one again; I went through and jammed the key in the lock; it clicked shut.

Within seconds I had reached the outside of the first door. I couldn't have beaten him by more than a few seconds; the lock clicked as he pulled on the handle. I doubled up, winded by the running, to which I wasn't accustomed, and the wound. He wrenched at the handle and banged at the door, but it held. It was old-fashioned and solid. He rammed it half a dozen times, then rammed the other one.

I sank to the ground, clutching my arm all the time, until it occurred to me to do something about it. I still couldn't see anything, but it was burning now, burning sharply and strongly, and the only thing I could do was tie the two handkerchiefs I found in my pocket onto the arm around the wound; I was hot and sticky there, but as I cooled, the sweat on me began to freeze. I just had to pray that the cut wasn't too deep or too wide, and that I wouldn't lose too much blood. I didn't know. I couldn't see. I feared I was going to faint.

Then I heard his voice, his soft whining voice, brittle with anger. "How are you Harry? How's your arm? I cut it long and deep: you'll be getting faint soon from the cold and loss of blood. I can imagine it dripping out there. You think you've been clever, don't you, locking me up in here? Well, I'll get out. And what will you do? If you survive the bleeding tonight, I'll come after you. There's no hope for you. Little copycat. Thought you could get in on my act, did you? Well, I'm quite comfortable in here. I'm prepared to wait. You can't keep me here forever."

He babbled on for some time in this vein. I was freezing cold by now, and my arm had gone completely numb, a massive throbbing pain coursing through the shoulder. I tried to feel it gingerly, and I could feel the shirt and jacket and handkerchiefs caked with blood. It seemed to me that it had dried. My head was feeling clearer now; perhaps he hadn't cut me as badly as he thought he had.

I said, "Ted, there's a tape recorder in there. I want you to confess your crimes, all of them. When you've finished, there's a coil of string. Tie it around the recorder, and lower it out of the window. Tell me when you're about to do so, and I'll collect it."

There was a high-pitched giggle. "Don't be so silly. Why should I confess?"

"Because you're not going to get out until you do. I don't mind if it takes days."

The giggle again. "A tape recorder. How ironic. That was what led to your downfall, wasn't it, Harry? Strange the faith you put in simple mechanical objects." He was silent for a while after that.

Then the crashing began. He crashed into the door, both doors, several times. I heard him pound with his infernal hammer, hack at the woodwork of the door with his knife—or whatever other instrument he was holding. "I wouldn't break the window," I told him. "You'll only be a lot colder." But he did, and I heard him banging the hammer on the bars. Then he started screaming. He screamed coherently to begin with: "Help! Let me out, let me out!" And then it just changed into a series of high-pitched shrieks and then a sort of low howling noise that degenerated still further into gasping sobs. It was piteous to listen to that awful quavering scream hanging on the mist across the moor, eddying from an empty house to ears that couldn't hear it. If anyone heard, I thought ruefully, they would turn and run.

After it became clear he wasn't going to confess easily, I decided to leave him. I was half frozen, and the ache in my arm was overpowering. He couldn't get out. I made my way out of the building with difficulty and got into the car. As I started the engine, I heard that terrible shriek again. I think he thought I was going to leave him to die.

I steered the Anglia down through the dark. As the car warmed up, I began to feel relief mixed with pain, as the wound began to feel less numb. I found the stream on the moor, which was icy cold, and with difficulty peeled the handkerchiefs off and bathed the wound. It had stopped bleeding: it was wide, a great gash across my arm, but not, I think, too deep. I put on the duffle jacket I carried in the back of the car, which made me less conspicuous, and made a makeshift sling with the arm of my jacket underneath it. Then I drove into Princetown village as dawn began to break. There was a café just outside the village. I went in there, and at that time in the morning the men were bleary-eyed with sleep. No one looked at me. I helped myself to three coffees and a plate of eggs and bacon which tasted like something heavenly. I began to feel sorry for the wretch I had left behind. But he had felt no pity for his victims.

Feeling a little better and much warmer, although the pain was as intense as ever, I drove back to the house. It looked more bleak and forbidding than ever through the gaps in the mist, and it was eerily silent. I went in through the cellar feeling apprehensive. Suppose he had got out? At least I would be able to see him now. I climbed the stairs warily, keeping an eye about me, passing through the doorways quickly. When I reached the room, there was a great red stain outside the door. My heart stopped, until I realised it was my old blood, not his. I knocked. "Ted, I'm back. Have you done what I asked you to?"

There was no sound, nothing from beyond the door. I peered through the keyhole, but it had a small field of vision. There was no sign of him. Perhaps he had got out; I looked about me nervously. I said, "I've just had breakfast. Eggs and bacon and coffee. It made me feel a lot better. You can have some too, if you do what I asked you to. Be sensible, Ted. You're not going to get out otherwise."

A low moan sounded from the other side of the door. "Let me out. Please. I don't like being locked up. Let me out." It was like a child speaking.

"Not unless you record that tape."

"I've done it." My heart leapt.

"Then lower the tape recorder from the window."

"Then you'll let me out?" There was suspicion in his voice.

"I promise." I went downstairs, through the cellar, to the other side of the house, beneath the back window. The ground was heavy with dew from the night mists. There was a little pile of glass on the ground where he had broken the window. Then I saw the little machine descending slowly. When it had reached the ground, the string was dropped contemptuously after it. I picked it up and took it with me back into the house into the large shuttered drawing room. I sat in a corner and played it.

The voice was strained with cold and hatred. "Oh, you think you're so clever, doing this to me, don't you? You think you've solved all your problems? Well, I've got news for you. You haven't. Of course I killed all the harlots they said I did. I, Ted Baines, killed ten girls between September last year and today. I admit it; I'm proud of it. I am the Hammer. But I want to point out that there was one murder in which I took no part, committed by one Harry Denham; the victim was Eileen DuBois, a prostitute of 33 Querchmore Road. I was there; I saw it. Afterwards I performed some surgery on the corpse, because I was tempted. But he killed her, by knocking her to the ground, and deserves to go down a long time for it. Wouldn't it be funny if we shared the same cell?

"So, Harry, your troubles are just beginning. If you condemn me, you condemn yourself. And that isn't all. You are condemned. You are condemned in your own horrible, scheming, copying mind. You killed a person. Doesn't that make you think, don't you have any remorse for your victim? You're a murderer, just like me. It doesn't matter that you only did it once, while I struck ten times. We are cut from the same cloth, you and I. Once the Rubicon is crossed there is no going back. You have inflicted death and life now is cheap for you.

"In fact, you could easily do it again, because you accepted it with so little trouble. When I first killed, Harry, I was desolate. I was terribly, terribly unhappy. I nearly had a breakdown. I didn't kill again for six months. You accepted it as easily as that; as easily as I did after I had killed three times, when my feelings were no longer engaged, when I realised that girls that behaved like that were pieces of meat, ripe for the butcher's knife. I felt no pity for them after that, only pleasure. I had a cleaning mission: by killing, I was redeeming the world: blood and sacrifice are always at the centre of any religion. I had a mission to purify. Anyway, you felt no pity after your killing. No pity—to the extent that you were prepared to falsify evidence to convict me. To hurt another person. That's what I call real ruthlessness, real callousness. You're the murderer, not me. You know that in your own heart. We're in the same club. We're of the same stripe. Only you're worse than me.

"I can talk to you like a mate, then. It's fun doing the girls in, isn't it? The crack when their skulls break—that's fun too, isn't it? You should know. It gives one a special feeling, doesn't it, squeezing the life out of one of them whores, them little tarts? I enjoy it, you enjoy it, we should swap stories over a pint, go into business together. You are like me, you are me."

I switched the damn thing off. I couldn't take it anymore. The cold sweat had got me again. I couldn't listen to his sick, mocking tone. I wanted to dash the damn recorder to the ground. I had never heard anything so sick. I stumbled to my feet and went over to the corner of the room and leaned

my arm against the wall. I wanted to get out into
the fresh air, away from his sick mind. As I staggered for support, I hit my elbow against the wall,
and the surge of pain was agonising. I realised why
I had been struck cold by his words. It was that he
was right. I was a monster like him, I had crossed
the point of no return, I couldn't ever purge what I
had done.

A surge of black self-hatred ran through me. I
wanted to kill him, and I wanted to kill myself. We
were both better off dead. And in that instant I
realised that my hatred for him and my hatred for
myself were one and the same. We were the same
person. He was right.

Half blinded by pain, I found myself struggling
up the staircase. Up and up it seemed to go, in my
despairing self-hatred. And when I reached the top,
it didn't surprise me to find the door of the room
open and the wood around the lock splintered
where he had hacked at it, maybe for hours, with
the sharp end of his hammer. The room was
empty. He was loose. He might be waiting for me,
watching for me. But it didn't matter now.

I struggled back down the stairs, not caring
about the noise I was making, half expecting a
shape to leap from the shadows. I reached the bottom floor of the large, gloomy, empty house. There
was no sound. I hesitated before going into the cellar, because it was so dark. As I walked through it,
I half expected the flash of a blade, the crack of a
hammer. None came.

I climbed up the steps into the yard, into the
refreshing, bitter, damp cold. There was still a little mist about, but I could see some way ahead. An

impulse told me to cross the moor to where, five hundred yards away, the lip of the cliff lay. Would I have the courage? I didn't know. If he was about, self-inflicted death was better than death at his hands. I knew it had to end now.

I stumbled across the tufts of moor heather towards the lip of the precipice. I turned once or twice to see if he was following, but there was nothing in my field of vision. To destroy him I had to destroy myself. I was evil, cast in the same mould as the Hammer. I stumbled towards that edge, to where I knew the soft ground would give way to rock and open air and sweet nothingness. Soon I would know freedom. It had been madness for me to try and capture a murderer by myself, as I had. I should have ended it all earlier. I was the monster, I was like him, I was the Hammer.

Then the mist parted and I found the ground dropping away under my feet. Just down a short green slope was the cliff. Seen from up here, it was a void, a precipitous slide of rock hurtling down hundreds of feet into the mist: I thought I could see grass at the bottom, but it was hard to make anything out for sure. The sight of that emptiness made me giddy. I had to stop myself from falling backwards into the grass, from succumbing to the blind panic which told me to run away. And then my eye caught sight of something.

At first I thought it was a rag stuck to the rock. But as I peered a little closer, it took human form: you could tell there were two legs, two arms spread-eagled out on the rock; part of its clothing fluttered in the breeze. Another suicide. It seemed incredible. I began to inch forward, out of sheer curiosity and fascination. I reached where the edge led down to a straight cleft in the rock, where I could balance myself with difficulty and look straight down on the body.

With a start, I realised who it was: his glazed, impersonal look, his bared teeth were as they were when he was alive. But his eyes could see no longer. He seemed almost comfortable in death, as though there had always been something deathlike about his eyes and his movements and his slight build in life. He was quite dead, that was evident from he way his eyes were open and his body grotesquely positioned on the rock.

I climbed back up the grassy bank. I could not believe it, could not accept what I had seen. I had helped, after all, to rid the world of this monster. Had he merely lost his way and fallen? Or had he killed himself? I would never know. I thought the latter was more probable; that after his escape from the room, some kind of remorse must have seized him, remorse for the victims whom he had boasted about in the tape—or it might have been just cowardice, the fear of what would happen to him if I got the tape to the police. He had known, as I had known, that he was at the end of the road, that for him there was no way out.

I sank to the ground, the mossy wet ground over which the mist drifted lazily about. I was oblivious to the cold, to the numbing sensation in my arm. I had been saved. A new life could begin. My persecution was no more. I could take out my money, go to a new town, begin again, maybe find another, better job. A dawn beckoned. It was hard to believe that my night was over.

I was surprised that I did not feel more elated; instead there was a feeling of emptiness. I thought that my preoccupation with him, with getting rid of him, had become my raison d'être for the past few weeks. Without him, without my job, without Mummy, there was nothing much to do, no further purpose.

I should kick myself. Why was my deliverance being accompanied by depression? I could not understand my mood. It remained for me to take the tape to the police, to explain everything, to take them to the body. They might not believe me at first; but I was sure that the evidence would convince them in the end. It would be sticky for a time; but I assumed his tools of murder were still on him, and in his house. I would have to decide whether to confess to my hand in Eileen's death, or whether to edit the tape first; best not to, surely, because if it seemed to be doctored they might consider the evidence had been tampered with. I could say it was his invention, or I could confess and hope to be let off with a manslaughter charge. It had been an accident. They would be so elated to be rid of the Hammer that I felt sure that all problems would resolve themselves. So what was this deep despair about?

I pulled myself up, wet from the ground, and went over to the Anglia and started it up. I knew then what the despair was about, and I had a glimpse of what I would have to do.

It was the second time I had been to that cemetery in a month. This time I watched the funeral from afar. It was a pathetic affair, as pathetic as Mummy's had been. Just seven mourners: a couple who must have been her parents, an elderly man who looked slightly similar to him, another couple, probably neighbours, and the widow and her child.

She looked lonely, bewildered, and lost, from a distance. She seemed distracted as she walked behind her husband's coffin, as though she couldn't concentrate, being steered by helping hands down the direction the procession was taking. Her little daughter was restless; she didn't look sad; I imagined she hadn't known her father too well, because he was out so much of the time; or maybe she just didn't get on with him. In my brief experience of him, there was a chilly kind of shyness there that would not have encouraged intimacy with children. The little girl was close to her mother though; when she wasn't wandering off, she clutched her hand and her skirt protectively.

I didn't go too close because I noticed the two policemen in plain clothes watching from a distance. The death had rated a few lines in the paper, that was all: a walker had fallen off the Grampian rocks. Foul play was not suspected. The implication was that he had committed suicide. All the same, I suspected the police would want to keep an open verdict. They had no idea that the man they had expended so many hours of police manpower upon was being buried, quietly, unrecognised.

I had made my decision: I would tell them nothing; they had proved so clueless in the chase, they deserved to be cheated at the end of it. Their prey would elude them; the murders would simply stop, and they would never know, just as they had never been able to close their file on the original Jack the

Ripper. My main motive in all this was to spare her and her daughter. Why cause more suffering for the innocent? Life would be bleak enough for her as it was. That she knew nothing of her husband's activities I was absolutely convinced. Why condemn her to live knowing that her husband had been a mass murderer? Why condemn her child, a total innocent, to life as the child of a monster? They had to be spared. Their suffering would otherwise be lifelong.

I strolled away from the cemetery, the sun a washed-out ball in a slight mist. It was cold. I picked up an evening paper, and I thought I would go and get a pint to cheer me up on my way back to the cheerless motel I was staying at. I had time on my hands now. I could rest. I was no longer being pursued by a madman. I sat down at the motel bar and unfurled the paper. A banner headline; IS THE HAMMER DEAD?, was blazoned across the top.

A chill ran through me. I read the story beneath it with a sense of futility and despair: she would not be spared after all. That scatty, rather endearing creature would be mentally destroyed and her daughter warped for life. The story spoke of police suspicions that a recent death might not have been unconnected with the Hammer murders, and the police expectation that no further murders would be committed. The language was curious, but I assumed they must have found the hammer and the knife beside his body. There were no specifics, but the piece spoke of "mysterious circumstances" surrounding the death, including the discovery of a patch of blood near the scene of the crime.

Depressed, desolated by the crisis about to over-

take two young lives, I downed pint after pint. At
length, I summoned up the courage to do what I
knew I must do.

The van was stainless steel, hard and impersonal,
and bare. The window was meshed and barred. I
was being whisked through the streets at enormous
speed, and the sirens were ringing like screams
from hell. The two men on either side of me were
short, burly, unsmiling. Each was chained to me by
handcuffs. The cuffs had been on for more than a
day, and my wrists were sore. None of the policemen spoke to me; it was a silent journey. I could
feel the tension of the hatred and contempt they
felt for me. There was not a speck of human sympathy present. Any one of them would have happily killed me, then and there.

They hadn't even had the pleasure of squeezing a
confession out of me. I had gone in there and con-
fessed to Inspector Prescott, there and then. He
had sat quietly, chain-smoking as usual, while two
officers took notes. Occasionally he raised his eyes
and looked at me, as I told him the whole terrible
story. Of how I had been driven to kill the girls to
clean up the streets of the town. Of the passion
with which I hated them, and the pleasure with
which I carved them up. Of how I had felt remorse
only after the last one, realised suddenly that she
was a human being as well as a whore; of how there
would be no more killings now that I had surren-
dered myself. I had been calm and controlled as I
told him, and although I could read in his eyes the
deep ingrained scepticism of a policeman, he had

no choice but to believe. The circumstantial evidence pointed that way.

And there would be no more killings. He had been cheated out of the pleasure of apprehending me; but his life would not be made a misery by the discovery of a new body every couple of months.

At the end of it all, he said, "You've made my life hell for a long time, Harry. And I'd have bet my shirt that it wasn't you."

I smiled thinly. "I let you down, didn't I?"

He and the policemen gazed at me with a peculiar look of revulsion, hatred, and curiosity for something beyond comprehension, capable of an evil they couldn't begin to understand. I was someone who had passed beyond the extremities of human behaviour. I was to know that look for the rest of my life.

I had been given my own cell, to keep me apart from the other prisoners, which I appreciated. It was actually quite comfortable, although very boring. There was nothing to do there. A defence lawyer had been assigned to me—quite an eminent one, I believed, because in all the big trials they took care to give the impression that justice was being done. He was a shifty little man, who didn't look me in the eye, but glanced at me quickly when I wasn't looking at him.

He asked me how I wanted to plead. I said guilty. He said, "You're very wise. It'll save a lot of time. And after your confession you don't stand a chance of getting off. The court may appreciate you're saving them time." He didn't sound very hopeful.

Now I was being rushed to committal proceedings. The whole hypocritical farce of justice had to be got out of the way. To the guilty, it was all just a charade. I supposed it provided some hope for the innocent. I wanted to get it over with as quickly as possible. The van tore around bends, barely diminishing its speed until it screeched to a halt with a jerk that nearly threw us out of our seats, and made the handcuffs on my wrist hurt most painfully. If my captors had any sympathy, they didn't show it.

"Let's go," said one gruffly, tugging me to my feet with the handcuffs. I became aware of a sound outside: it was a loud, cacophonous, jeering sound: a lynch mob. "Christ, look at that," said one of the policemen, glancing out of the window.

"You can't blame 'em," said another gruffly. "Come on, let's get it over with. Want a blanket?" he asked me. I didn't understand what he meant at first. Then I realised he meant one over my head. It didn't matter to me either way. I had no relatives or friends to be hurt. I shook my head. He looked at me a moment, then said, "Suit yourself." They opened the back doors, and I felt the sudden rush of cold air after the stuffiness of the van. Then I was being pulled forward.

Mayhem followed. I was propelled by the two men into a ring of about twenty policemen, tough, broad-shouldered men trying hard to keep away a huge wedge of screaming, furious women yelling every obscenity I had ever heard, unintelligible in the froth of their hatred. In front of the police, a rabble of television photographers and cameramen were snapping away, as my men tried to push me through them. I hardly knew what was happening, there were so many people. The cameras were clicking like ticker-tape machines, and behind them the awful shouting went on. As we pushed through I saw a policeman being kicked over and his helmet falling to the ground. And then rough hands had grabbed my collar, words were being screamed at me, nails were scratching at me. I closed my eyes briefly and when I opened them I could feel the gashes beneath them. A bulky woman of sixty with glasses and a furious face was being pulled away; I was pulled by the detectives in a rush into the building. Suddenly I felt something wet on my face; and then the spitting began. It could only have lasted thirty seconds before we were inside and the doors clanged behind, but half of my face was running with the spittle and great gobs of it rolled down my shirt and jacket.

Inside, the police sighed heavily. "Here, clean yourself up," said one, offering me a handkerchief. I dabbed myself. Someone fetched a plaster for my scratches. "I'll wear the blanket on the way out," I said wearily. He gave me an ironical look.

They led me into court. Instantly the public gallery, filled with people, erupted. Shouts and jeers interrupted the court. "Clear the gallery, clear the gallery!" cried the chairman of the magistrates. After they had left, the proceedings took only a few minutes. I was remanded in custody while the police made further investigations. My lawyer didn't apply for bail.

I was led out. The sergeant handed me the blanket; I looked him in the eye. "That's all right, thank you." He looked at me hopelessly. I was subjected to the same venom on my way back to the Black Maria; but I held my head high. In my mind's eye was a vision of that widow and her daughter. I had adopted them, I was their benefactor. No one would ever do them a better turn.

For the first time since Eileen's death, the shadow over me had lifted. I had a new responsibility now that my mother had passed away. A new responsibility that released me. I could look the world in the face. I was doing something better than I had ever done before.

ABOUT THE AUTHOR

Jason Trench is a widely traveled journalist.
Brought up in Britain, he is married, with one son.
The Hammer is his second novel for the Crime Club.

TREUCH, JASON
THE HAMMER
MYSTERY

MAI

MAY 1 1 1990